The Geography of Water

Mary Emerick

UNIVERSITY OF ALASKA PRESS, FAIRBANKS

Text © 2015 University of Alaska Press
All rights reserved

University of Alaska Press
PO Box 756240
Fairbanks, AK 99775-6240

Library of Congress Cataloging-in-Publication Data

Emerick, Mary.
  The geography of water / by Mary Emerick.
    pages cm
  ISBN 978-1-60223-270-9 (pbk. : alk. paper)—ISBN 978-1-60223-271-6 (e-book)
  I. Title.
  PS3605.M45G46 2015
  813'.6—dc23
                              2014049535

Cover and interior design Jen Gunderson, 590 Design LLC
Cover image: Julien L. Balmer

This publication was printed on acid-free paper that meets the minimum
requirements for ANSI / NISO Z39.48–1992 (R2002) (Permanence of Paper for
Printed Library Materials).

for my parents, who always believed

Lynn, who gave me the title

and to those who shared their hearts and stories with me
along the coast of Baranof Island in Southeast Alaska.
You will never be forgotten.

One

When my father left on his hunting trips, my mother and I would come out of our hiding places. We would scamper like mice through the empty lodge, throwing open the windows to erase the smell of men. We would fill up the damp air with our own voices, losing little pieces of our hearts with doomed Janis Joplin, the volume knob turned up past ten. We would surrender like drowning to afternoon sleep in beds that were not our own. We would eat, finally, sitting down like normal people, peaches sliding down our throats, each swallow almost too sweet to bear. We would stretch ourselves big in a world that usually forced us to be small.

Always we were as close as sisters. We shared everything, even the oversized claw-foot tub that my father had shipped on the barge from Seattle. I knew that some would think it was strange, a mother and daughter so close. The clients told us it was so. They shot searching glances at us, as if we were very different from them, living here miles from any other family. Perhaps we were. We had no barometer with which to compare.

But my mother and I were just alike. We even looked alike, the same bright hair and light eyes, no trace of my father's darkness about me. We were twins, almost. Except for one thing: I was stronger than she was. My mother was like a candle, thin and bright. It would not take much to blow her out. "Next year, I'll be eighteen," I told her. "An adult. I could leave." I said this, but I felt cruel. The only way out was by floatplane or boat, how could she ever go?

All season long a parade of puffy men passed through the lodge, hunting clients. They were stiff in new rubber boots and creased Carhartts. They tracked in mud and dribbled Copenhagen on the rugs. They were from cities, places like Dallas and Pittsburgh.

My father served them brandy and courage. He told stories of near death in the mountains and on the sea: bear attacks, sixty-foot falls from slippery ridges, and bivouacs in the fog. The men listened, drinking quickly. They laughed loudly and often to cover up their fear. Muggers, carjackers, they thought they knew. In this world, our world, they were blind. My father was the star they followed.

When they left, my mother and I scrubbed their rooms. We bundled the sweaty sheets and wove sightlessly with our towering burdens down the stairs to the laundry. We mopped and steam cleaned, erasing any trace of them. We sank to the floor after the last one, our skin smelling of lemons. "This is the way it should always be," she said. "Just us, scoured clean." I knew that she did not really mean it. She longed for my father's return.

When my father was home, his smoker's cough punctuated the hours. We could track him by the sound of it. We watched his moods like the weather. If the hunt had gone well, he was liquored up and expansive. "Girls! Where are you?" he bellowed, shedding his layers of rain gear and camouflage. He was charming then, waltzing us across the great room. It was easy to think it would always be this way. If something went wrong, though, a gut shot or another boat anchored in his favorite bay, he stormed through the lodge, brows drawn down. Either way, the air was uneasy, ready to turn at any moment. My mother and I had the scars to prove it.

We compared them, sitting in the claw-foot tub.

"Scar from falling into the kitchen table," she said, lifting a leg out of the bubbly water. "Burn from brushing up against the stove."

"Dislocated shoulder," I countered. "Black eye, twice."

She lifted her hair, a waterfall of gold. "You know I try to protect you. He would never hurt you. It is always by accident."

"I know it." All of my war wounds came from trying to save her, running downstairs barefoot, an innocent bystander caught in the scuffle. Each time, an accident, a mistake. The same excuse for her. She got in the way. He was hungry. Tired. He never meant it.

When I asked, she said that men had anger hidden deep inside, like lava at the earth's hidden heart. Women had to be careful, she said. It was up to us to keep the peace.

Nobody would blame me if I snuck aboard the supply barge the next time it pulled in. But how could I leave her? Even though I threatened to go, I could not imagine it. She would shrink without me, her ribs and spine stretching her skin even tighter than they did now.

I had started to think that she did not want to be saved.

She sighed, rising from the tub. "There are so many good things about him. You will understand when you are older."

But I did not believe her. I was in love with our assistant guide. Sam was older than I was, nearly twenty-five, but like my mother said, you couldn't choose who you loved. The heart wants what it wants, she said. I watched him through the windows as he loaded the skiffs. He was everything my father was not.

I thought that he might know that I loved him, because he talked to me on the dock while he cleaned fish. Blood flowed in a sheet as he filleted halibut. As he worked, he kept an eye on the lodge. "Better go," he warned me. "It's not a good day today." Like us, he charted the way my father's moods ebbed and flowed like the tides of our bay. He called me Buddy, as though we were in this together.

He never called me by my name: Winnie, real name Winchester. I was named after the rifle my father carried. In the evenings he cleaned and oiled it, pushing the white patch through the muzzle until it came out spotless. It was a serious gun, with power behind it. It was a name I was not sure I could live up to.

It rained, mist blanketing the bay down below the tree line. We were cut off from the world when the storms rolled in. "We are our own planet," my mother said. She steeped strong, earthy tea the color of coal. Her face was serene. She loved the ocean as much as she loved me.

We put on our rain bibs and boots and walked the estuary. My mother added up the ways a person could survive out here. "Beach asparagus," she said. "Salmonberries, fat and juicy. Goose tongue." We opened our mouths and let the rain fall down our throats. She had shown me how to start a fire by peeling the dry inner bark of the hemlock. I could fix a kicker, tie a bowline, and gut a deer. "You have to be able to survive," she said. "This is not like any other place. Nobody will save you here."

Anybody who had lived here long enough knew the names of the dead. My father's old guide, the one before Sam, an unsteady man named Roger, his breath a fiery stew of bourbon and cigars, drowned crossing the strait, his skiff found washed up on Harbor Island. The youngest McCarthy, the son of the man who brought us supplies on the barge, was killed in an explosion aboard his long-liner. And Uncle Dean in the pilot's seat of his DeHavilland Beaver, lost on his way back to the lodge to pick up clients, never seen again.

Death smelled like fish. Salmon were running in the creek. They were decaying as they swam, their mouths hooking, eyes milky, the humps on their backs growing pronounced. "Humpies are almost done," I said. "That means only one more bear hunt. Nothing after that until April when the spring hunts start."

"This winter will be better," my mother said like she believed it. But I was old enough to think that nothing would change. Sam would not stick around during the off-season. He headed south to Panama or Peru to pick up a deckhand job for a few months. In the really cold winters, the bay iced over and our boats were held fast at the dock. Planes could not land and the barge would not attempt to break through. It would be only us.

My mother pointed. A humpback whale breached in the bay entrance. The water closed over its sleek tail. Soon the whales we saw would leave for Hawaii to give birth in the tropics. They would not be back until months had gone by.

We turned our backs on the beach and climbed through brushy cypress toward the muskeg. Generations and generations of bears had traveled here, each one stepping in the same footprints. We did the same, setting our feet in the wide depressions.

"Let's go visit James Tucker's grave," I suggested. Our boots sank into the spongy living carpet. I liked muskegs because they were open and straightforward. What you saw was what you got. The rest of the forest was shaded and deep. Huge trees loomed like strangers. Anything could creep up on us there.

We did not know who James Tucker was, but someone loved him once. His marker was a flat silver pane. We found it by chance when we stopped here, my boot striking something hard in the sphagnum moss. We scraped it clean, but all that was engraved was his name.

We made up stories about him. One day he was a bootlegger, ambushed for his case of rum. Another time he was a baby, born in secret to one of the Scottish cannery workers who used to live down the coast when the herring were plentiful.

"James Tucker," I started the game. "I wonder who he was."

My mother thought. "He's someone who wanted what he couldn't have," she said. "He's someone who died from a broken heart."

People had lived here before us. We had found the mossy remains of Tlingit longhouses in the beach fringe, sagging screened pens from fox farms out on the islands, an abandoned cannery squatting in head-high salmonberry a few bays over, pilings marching out into the intertidal zone. Sometimes glass floats, once attached to fishing nets, washed up onto our beach, carried by the Japanese current. Somehow they escaped the teeth of the cliffs and arrived whole.

People would live here after us, too.

We looked out over the wide, wide sea.

"The next landfall is Japan," my mother said.

"Could I swim there?" I asked. It's a question I asked her once as a little girl, and she still liked to hear it. This story was part of the sinew that bound us together.

"You'd float on your back," she began. "Your hair would turn to kelp, your eyes to abalone. Your bones would curve and your skin would become slippery. They say that all the whales in the ocean sing the same song. This time you would understand the words. You'd learn all the secrets the whales have to tell."

"And then what would happen?"

"And then I'd find you," she said. "I would dive into the water, holding on to your back. We would swim through the ocean, blowing bubbles. You wouldn't be afraid, because I would never leave you." She reached for my hand. "Say your part. Say it."

"I won't leave you. I already said. I *promised.*"

"I know," she said. Her eyes brightened. "We've got nine more days until the hunt is over. Let's row out past the islands, way out where the puffins are. We'll anchor in the deep water and pull up our crab pots. The hunt will go fine, and things will be better, the very best they've ever been."

I wanted to believe her, I really did. But it was getting harder and harder. I saw more now than I used to, a sullen undercurrent in our lives previously hidden.

She cupped my chin in hers. "Winnie, you're going to have a brother in the spring."

I caught my breath. Of all the things she could have told me, this is the one I least expected. "How do you know?"

"I can feel him swimming under my skin," she told me. "Tell me you're happy."

She lay back in the muskeg, a yellow-haired elf. Her rain bibs swallowed her up. "This will make all the difference, you'll see. We'll take him everywhere we go. We'll show him how to dig for scallops and which mushrooms are safe to eat. We'll teach him everything there is to know."

"Will we show him the good hiding places?" I whispered. But she did not answer. Her eyes were closed; maybe she had gone to sleep.

Far below us, the ocean tried to eat the rocks that guarded our bay. I looked for the whale but it was gone. Maybe it was deep underwater, singing a haunting melody. I liked to think of it calling to a loose skein of whales that swim south together. They would stay together no matter what, through the changing of the tides, the wind and the rain.

Back in the lodge, we sat long into the night. The rain slapped its way past the eaves, marked the windows, dripped onto the ground. The sound of running water was almost something I could understand; I thought if I tried hard enough I could hear words in it.

She drank wine the color of the blood that stained the docks after the killing. She drank even though she should not, because of the baby. I had never been able to tell her what to do. I could see the wine spreading through her, filling her fingers, her bare toes.

She talked, the wine talked.

"He drains me dry," she said. "He needs so much air, there is none left for me."

I thought of the halibut we pulled from far in the sea, how their whole bodies bellowed with their breath before we clubbed them.

"How do you leave someone like him?" she asked. "He is like a bear, both wonderful and terrible at the same time."

This made sense to me, because over the years my father had grown to resemble the bears he hunted. He was as dark as she was light, eyes with no bottom to them, black hair dense and thickly furred across his chest and head.

There was one difference though. I had been around bears long enough to know that unlike what the clients thought, they were mostly predictable. It was humans who were not. With my father, you never knew which man you were going to get.

Rain had many sounds. Because it could rain up to six feet a year in this forgotten corner of southeast Alaska, we were used to its backdrop. Days with sun felt alien, too bright. The rain held us in its arms—a drawstring, closing us up. The nearest people lived five miles down the coast, in a place called Floathouse Bay. On many days it might as well be fifty miles, it felt that far. I thought that I could live and die here without anyone noticing.

Outside, the light had long since gone out. In September, we were losing precious minutes of the daylight that lasted nearly all night in June. We were sliding into another winter, without clients, without Sam, just the three of us in our iced-in bay. I started to feel a little desperate.

The rain continued. I could feel its steady hum as I lay in bed, adding up one more safe night, like I could stack the deck in our favor. I thought about the baby, a secret for now between my mother and me, a reason she would pick to stay. My brother would be one more anchor to hold us here, one more way we would lose our wings, until the thought of flight was just something we made up one rainy night when the house was silent and there was nothing to hold us back.

The weather changed overnight. The rain had turned to snow up high, frosting the trees, and a north wind blew across the bay, whipping it up into a little chop. A storm was coming; we could feel the drop in pressure, pushing us low and heavy toward the earth.

The bears sensed it too. Instead of feeding in the stream they lay low in their day beds, waiting for it to pass.

"They'll cut the hunt short," my mother said, watching.

Because this was private land, not owned by the Forest Service, my father often cabled a line across our bay to keep the tourists out. We saw their boats pass by, wide-bodied white ships with names like *Wilderness Adventurer*. In years past they sent inflatable zodiacs in, bristling with fly rods, until my father fired shots in the air and they retreated. The only boat that came in now was the barge, dropping off our mail, my schoolwork, and groceries. Floatplanes brought in the clients and their wives. Everyone else knew better.

We pulled on our rain gear and our boots and walked down the ramp to the dock. It was low tide, and all the sea creatures waited for water. Purple sea stars lay sprawled in wet clumps among the rocks, and translucent moon jellies were pulsing bubbles. Clams, buried in the sand, squirted streams of water high into the air. The barnacles crackled and popped. Everything was alive, moving and breathing.

Under the curtain of fog we saw that the bears were back, splashing in the stream, catching humpies. They weren't the big boars; those were wary, easy to spook, and didn't come out until it was nearly dark. The ones out there now were teenagers. They ate in an uneasy truce, occasional charges and growls keeping each other in line. As they ate, they dragged the salmon up into the trees. Later, as the remains rotted, nitrogen seeped into the soil, a life-giving force that kept the trees fat. Bears and trees, locked together in an endless dance.

I knew these bears, had seen them all my life. I recognized them by their little differences: this one had darker fur than the others, another's ear was torn. Even though I was not allowed to name the bears, my father would not let his clients hunt here. He spent hours watching them. "I'm trying to think like a bear," he told us. He moved closer and closer, crouched behind a rock, until he blended in. If I did not pay attention, I mistook him for one of them.

"I don't want him to come back," I broke the silence. "It's better, just the two of us. You know it is."

She leaned down. "Look, beach glass." She placed it in my hand, a sliver of pale blue.

"Where do you think it came from?" she asked. This was another game we played, guessing where the tides had been. This piece had been pummeled by the waves for so long that its sharp edges were smoothed over. It had been changed into something else completely.

When I did not answer, she said, "England, maybe, the white cliffs of Dover. A lonely woman in a long red scarf, writing a message in a bottle for someone to find, only the bottle is lost in a storm. This is all that is left."

She waited for my answer. Always before I had given her one.

"We can take the skiff and go down to Floathouse Bay," I told her, finally saying it aloud. "They'll help us get away. We could go anywhere."

We looked out toward the ocean. Whitecaps marched in a solid line, big rollers fighting the flood tide. Out there it was what we called a confused sea, waves colliding from all four directions. I knew what that felt like because I felt it too, love and hate mixed up in a ball, rolling around loose inside my skin.

"Nobody's going anywhere," my mother said. But she hesitated; there was a crack in her armor.

"I know how to run the boat," I insisted. "We'll hug the shore. We have maps, and we have time."

She said nothing. She never did. This was a game too; we had played out the steps a million times. "I don't want to leave you," I said. "But I will. You know he won't ever change, no matter how often he promises us."

She had heard this before. Always before I chose her.

At the dock the skiff bounced in the chop. It was our oldest one, a Lund that was tippy and leaking. It had an unreliable motor and a bad gas line. Water pooled on its flat bottom and moss coated the railings. But it was a way out.

I pulled the starter cord and the motor rumbled into life. "Are you coming?" I held my breath. There were so many ways it could go.

I wanted to see it like this: My mother sitting up near the bow, looking for rocks. I would have one hand on the tiller, steering up and over the breakers. The five miles we had to travel would pass like a dream. The point that signaled Floathouse Bay would loom ahead, freedom and safety all in one.

Waiting, I looked across the bay. In the stream, the bears moved like the tides, a complex hierarchy of aggression and avoidance. The little ones were being chased out now. They moved back into the trees, the forest zipping them up.

My mother had already started back up the dock. She waited, her hood pulled up, hiding her face. "Come on, Winnie," she called.

I stood there, one foot in the boat, the other on the dock. Then I closed my eyes and chose.

Two

I had always thought that anger ran through all men like a slender thread, but if it was there in Isaiah and Birdman, I could not find it. From the first day I arrived in Floathouse Bay I hunted for that anger in them. I knew it had to be there, a red pulse waiting below the surface. I even tested it sometimes, just to finish the waiting for it, because the waiting was always worse. I tried leaving the shovel out to rust or sending the coffee cascading over the cup, little things that had sometimes caused my father to slam his fist down on the countertop.

If they knew they were being tested, neither man said so. Birdman placed the shovel back under the eaves; Isaiah mopped up the spill with a rag, humming. "Someone's got her head in the clouds today," he said, winking.

Finally I had to know. I thought of the volcano I had heard of way up north. People called it Redoubt, a hulk of what looked like lifeless stone but it was waiting, smoldering below the surface. Every lifetime it seemed to shake off sleep and belch out smoke and fire. Each time it caught people off guard, as if they had forgotten what lay beneath. Maybe Isaiah and Birdman were like that, a slow burn instead of a flame.

"Is it true that all men are angry?" I asked.

13

"Left all of my angry back in 'Nam," Isaiah said. He fussed with a set of marten traps on the dock. The only jeans I ever saw him wear were blotched with fish blood and held up by a section of parachute cord and a pair of suspenders. A logger's striped shirt, made for a slimmer man, stretched tight across his belly. His face was round as a moon, fringed by a wispy goatee the color of ginger. From the first, I thought I could see all of him down to a sweet core.

"Some men just have fault lines closer to the surface," he said, and I knew without asking that he meant my father was one of those men. "Some of us never have them at all."

I was coming to understand that there were different kinds of men in the world. Isaiah was as transparent as my father had been opaque. He bumbled through life in an eternal good-natured fog, misplacing his cheater glasses, forgetting to put back parts in the generator as he fixed it. He laughed with his whole body. It was hard to remember what anger was when I was around Isaiah.

Birdman was harder for me to read. Stooped in eternal pain, his body a coiled muscle, he guarded himself against me. For the first month I lived in Floathouse Bay, he did not say more than a handful of words, only sizing me up the way I had so often sized up the sea. His eyes missed nothing, not the tears I disguised as salt spray or the way I sometimes watched the path out to the ocean, waiting for someone who never came.

A line of cormorants sometimes perched on the floathouse docks, spreading their wings like ragged capes. I knew that they were underwater hunters, diving deep under the sea for food. After they came up from two hundred feet below the surface, they had to dry their wings before they could fly again. My mother used to call them the birds that swim.

"It's the best of both worlds," she used to say. "To be able to fly and to swim both." Watching them with her, I used to believe that they were luckier than we were, because they had two easy ways to escape.

Like the cormorants I was waiting for a sign. Floathouse Bay was born for waiting. You could wait all your life here because nothing ever changed. A tiny dimple in the coast that opened into a slender, dangerous throat, it gathered up the flood tide in its mouth and spit it back out every twelve hours. The *Coast Pilot*, the bible my father had followed like a religion, warned that a prudent mariner should give it a wide berth. Sucked almost dry in low tide, it was a place everyone left alone, everyone but the desperate.

It was a place that was made for me.

The tiny bay inside was peppered with saw-toothed rocks that submerged and reappeared with the pulse of the ocean, as deep and drawn out as one long sigh. Gulls worried the sea for the scraps of fish the men threw out in long arcs, squabbling and shrieking among themselves, rising up in indignant feathery clouds and then settling again a few feet away. Sometimes a sea lion broke the surface, a chunk of salmon in its jaws.

On the long, unending days, Isaiah worked to repair wide lacy nets to the beat of sixties rock tunes scratchily emerging from a transistor radio. Birdman tended plants in the greenhouse, its materials salvaged from the sea. Above everything the mountains marched in an endless cloak of green to sky the color of pavement.

In Floathouse Bay it was easy to believe that you could wait forever. When I looked into the mirror that the last woman to stay here had left, I was surprised to see that my hair had not turned silver, that wrinkles had not made a road map on my face. It seemed that long that I waited.

I was waiting too for the mosquito buzz of a boat, my mother's skiff rounding the cliffs that separated the bay from the ocean outside. Sometimes I could feel an invisible rope stretching through the miles and islands and bays that were between us. Throughout the long days ticking into dubious half nights at Floathouse Bay—the sun only a wrinkle on the horizon, barely setting at all—I listened for the sound of a motor, the sight of a kayak.

I waited, but nobody came. I knew that my mother had learned where I was. Ernie, who piloted the supply barge, was our coastal telegraph, and Isaiah had lived here long enough to know that a young woman staying with two older men in an isolated bay was unusual, even for this area where people kept to their own business. People would find out. People would talk. Ernie himself would carry the story all the way to Cape Deception, the far edge of land where two sides of the island came together in a splash of foam and tide.

Isaiah went out to meet the barge when I first came. He spent an hour with Ernie, floating in the chop, alluding to why I was there. I knew that he did not need to explain, but if he didn't give Ernie a story, Ernie would make up his own. Ernie knew what went on in Never Summer, the same way he knew when the couple at the fish weir split the sheets but were forced to stay on in a small hut until a floatplane could retrieve one of them in summer. He absorbed trouble like the air and later told everyone else about it, gossip his only reward for long days beaten up in the kidneys pushing the barge north.

At the same time, Ernie never took sides and quickly scooted away before being pulled in to the fight. He had told us in Never Summer once that the isolation of the coast turned people strange. They even looked different after enough months spent out here in the company of only a few others.

Down the coast near Split Point, he said, a crew at the archeo-logical site ran and hid, bush-fevered, when he pulled in after many months gone, only creeping out to retrieve the groceries after the barge had pulled away. The man and wife at the cannery instead desperately waved him in and plied him with muffins in an attempt to hear a new voice. Children with only parents for company were old souls, and the adults themselves either turned inward or had a streak of crazy. You never knew, Ernie said, which direction that isolation will make you swing.

So I knew that everyone in Never Summer Bay realized where I was. Maybe they thought I was waiting out the winter and would be back when the sedges poked their early heads up in the estuary. Spring was when everything came back to the coast. Even hope came back; hope that this season would be better than the last. When spring came, I thought, I would decide.

Stay or go? Staying was the easy course, and I was finding that I liked easy. The two old men moved in and out of the floathouse, letting me choose my own direction. "Whatever melts your butter. It don't hurt my feelings either way," Isaiah said with a grin, pulling on his floppy cowboy hat. Birdman stood hip deep in plants, snipping off leaves with long-handled scissors, nodding silently as I came to watch him work in the greenhouse. They both seemed to understand what I needed without me saying a word.

The men had called a group conference when it became clear that I was staying for more than a week. They set a few rules: I was to study each day using their motley collection of books. I was to get the papers to qualify for a high school diploma. And anytime I wanted to go back to Never Summer Bay, I could. The same rules held for moving on, hitching a ride with a passing long-liner to try my luck up north. If I got a wild hair to do that, Isaiah said, no worries. They wouldn't stop me.

This was a way station, they said, a place for the unlucky and the heartbroken. "The lonely hearts floathouse," Isaiah liked to call it with a gap-toothed grin. "It's a place to lick your wounds for a spell. Gather your courage and your strength." They would, he said, never ask me for my story unless I wanted to tell it. They would never have me make promises I could not keep.

The two men I found here living in a decrepit floathouse called themselves Isaiah and Birdman, but those were not their real names. What those were they wouldn't say. A rickety sailboat a woman had brought in years earlier was barnacled in at the shallow end of the bay and wouldn't move, and a flat-bottomed boat barely did. When they got liquored up they laughed big instead of hollering. They pole-vaulted over the campfire, their toes barely escaping the flames. They challenged each other to swim across the bay, their flaccid bodies turned to poetry as they dove and sliced through the water as smoothly as fish. They tended a still and a half dozen marijuana plants, thick-trunked as trees.

After they were used to me, they told stories late at night as the whiskey drained from their jam jars. The stories were of things that I could not understand: night running onto a tropical beach to slit sleeping throats and slipping back again, unnoticed. About the unbearable heaviness of the swampy air, the one crazy-eyed guy who grabbed a coral snake as a joke and then froze in fear with it dangling off his fingers, about mushroom-like rot festering between their sticky toes, about smoke from a thousand cigarettes. About collecting rainwater in cups and canteens and whatever else they had because they were always thirsty, chugging it down, not knowing then that they were drinking poison that had come from orange barrels. About seeing the blossom of red on friends' chests, losing the luck of the draw, as if it was all one big card game and they had picked the wrong suit. *Buying the farm. Kicking the bucket. Biting the dust. Pushing daisies. Taking a dirt nap.* They were rough cut and leather skinned, men who had lived hard lives and had the worn faces to prove it. They got their firewood from beach logs, their food from the land and sea, and never went to town, not ever.

They collected what they needed from the flotsam that washed up on the beaches. Every day they charted the weather, determining when the big spring tides would be, the extreme lows of fall, and planned out where to go to find the best bounty.

"You can get anything here, it's like a store," Isaiah liked to say. He showed me what he had found: glass fishing floats from Japan, Nike sneakers, and a flotilla of plastic bath toys. Each object was useful. Isaiah knew all about ocean currents. He once found an old globe, and he drew lines on it with his fingers to show me what would happen if a container fell off of a ship en route from Japan. "International date line, Alaska, Bering Sea," he said, tracing a path. "Years and years at sea, finally washing up here on the outer coast of Floathouse Bay."

I spent hours squatting on my heels watching him as he repaired marten traps. Unlike the lazy trappers farther down the coast, he said with disdain, the ones who used white plastic buckets that you could see for miles, he did it the old way, the better way. He tramped through the woods, sizing up the country. This could take hours, days of looking. He had all the time in the world. Finally he came to a halt at a place that was no different than any of the others we had passed by. "Here," he said, letting me hold the wooden box level while he nailed it to a spruce.

"Watch yourself," he warned me, setting the trip wire that would snap the animal's head instantly when it came to investigate the fish heads he left in the box.

I trailed behind him as we climbed higher to the muskeg. He stood tall and filled his lungs. "This is my homeland," he said, even though I knew he had been born in Arkansas. "Every day is a good day when I'm on the right side of the grass."

We stood for a moment looking over the wide expanse. More like river than land, a muskeg was a living sponge. Channels of murky water pulsed through its center, forming deep pools of brown-tinged water. My feet sank deep into a swampy yellow-and-green carpet of sphagnum moss and sedges. I recognized some of the plants that my mother had taught me: Labrador tea, Alaska cotton. Stunted lodgepole pines were taking over this meadow in a bloodless advance, slowly rooting into the wet soil and sucking up the moisture. In a hundred years it would be a forest. There would be no trace of what had been.

"I take it you aren't going back," Isaiah said. He took one of the marten traps from my arms. "Maybe could come up with some cash to send you north. Fairbanks, Delta. Almost eighteen, am I right? You could make a go of it up there."

In the open muskeg, I could see for miles. An unbroken carpet of musky-smelling green stretched toward the horizon, dozens of swamp plants woven together into a loose carpet. Distant, snow-covered mountains, the Fairweather Range, floated on the horizon. Far below I could even see the ocean and on it a toy-sized tugboat pushing a barge way out in the main channel.

Every time I thought about leaving this southeast coast, my mind seized up and I was unable to choose. I had read enough about the rest of Alaska to know that the interior of it lay like an enormous frozen sea caught in mid-curl. Tundra instead of tide, it was barren and empty and unsheltered from the wind that blew across it in great sheets. Fire raced through the twisted black spruce and deep snows fell in winter. It was a land of extremes, not moderated by our meandering Japanese current. Up there, there would be no sanctuary in the forest. Up there, you would be completely exposed.

Going down to the Lower 48, the place my father had always dismissed as "America," was even more precarious. I had heard from Ernie that you spent half your life in a car, staring at the taillights ahead of you, freeways in a spaghetti tangle. There were buildings that blocked out the sky and gardens tortured into tame shapes. There were smokestacks belching mustard-colored clouds that stained the sky. There were people everywhere, hurrying down the streets, shouldering you aside in their haste.

In the shiny magazines Ernie had sometimes brought me from town, women in America wore filmy skirts that wouldn't last a minute in Never Summer Bay. They painted their lips with sticky gloss the color of blood. They didn't wear stained Carhartts and pile their hair into a messy braid. Their hands, I was sure, were not dotted with hard calluses and scars from devil's club punctures, their feet not colorless from constant exposure to salt. In the pictures they strode down the street in heels stacked high, never needing a place to hide.

Even getting away from Alaska was a complicated web of boats and planes that seemed impossible to figure out. It was like the state wanted to hold us fast in its fist.

And there was this: leaving the coast meant leaving my mother behind.

Waiting in Floathouse Bay, I felt suspended in time and space. I floated in a bubble where the days were long and seamless.

"How come you want to hang out here with old guys like us?" Isaiah sometimes asked me. "We've used ourselves up, and you're still shiny new, like a penny that nobody's spent yet. Don't hide here forever, Winnie. There's a big world beyond this coast."

I knew there was. I studied the curve of the horizon stretching past what I knew. I saw the waves in one long train, coming from a place where people spoke an entirely different language. I whispered the names of bays I had only seen on the charts, names like one long poem: Kiksadi, Haida, Forgotten. Somewhere out there other people lived, people who didn't know my story. I could be anyone out there. The possibility made me dizzy. It was almost too much for me to comprehend. Better to stay and let the seasons make the decision for me.

Sometimes I started a letter to my mother: *Is everything still the same? Should I come home?* I discarded each one. She knew where I was. Because she did not send for me, she must be telling me something. *Stay where it is safe. Wait for a sign.*

Maybe my brother had taken my place. Maybe he was the one now who found the eggs the cormorants left in the cliffs. Maybe he was the one now who listened to the stories of the Vancouver expedition, men in tall ships years from home, who had climbed our bluffs to leave rock cairns there. Maybe he was the one who had broken the red thread, and peace had come to Never Summer Bay. I knew that I could find out by asking Ernie, who never backed down from answering a question, but in the end I did not want to know.

"Where would I go?" I asked. I wanted Isaiah to point me on a way that was easy and true. I wanted him to pull out a map and run his stout fingers down a black line. Instead his eyes avoided mine. His own path here had been crooked, a zigzag line across the country. He had barely made it here, he told me, arriving with a carpenter's belt and little else, escaping where he had come from by the skin of his teeth. There were states that wanted him; women who cursed him. He would not help me choose.

"Not that we want you to go," he said. "Kind of getting used to having you around, honest truth. But you know, others have come here before you. You won't be the last one to come. Only difference will be what you leave behind."

I knew about leaving things behind. Because I had left every-thing in Never Summer Bay, I wore the clothes of a woman named Honey. In her rush to get somewhere else, she had left piles of clothes behind. She was just a story now; Isaiah had no idea where she had gone or where she had come from before piloting the sailboat into Floathouse Bay. She had told a nearly unbelievable tale about waking in the night, her husband missing from the boat. Of driving in circles under a night sky prickled with stars, calling out his name. When she bargained for a ride on Ernie's barge and a hitch to Anchorage, she left the sailboat and all of her old life behind.

People left things behind all the time. My mother and I had found entire houses sometimes in other bays down the coast, hastily built hovels of driftwood and baling wire. They were listing and roofless, wind blowing tattered curtains in open windows. Drawn by a strand of gold pushing through marble, they had dug adits and built tracks for hauling carts down to the shoreline. They dynamited through rock and tunneled deep inside, far past where the sun could ever reach. At one time, my father had said, there were hundreds of people scratching out a living on this coast.

I had always wondered what happened to those people. Where had they gone? The gold they had worked so hard for dried up about midcentury; it was too tough to work and many must have drifted on to other places where life was easier. "Couldn't hack it," my father had dismissed them, rowing out to the deeper water where he could start the engine. "Not like us. We'll be here forever."

Whenever I pulled on Honey's clothes, I wondered where she was now. Did she dream of this place? Did she ever think of what she had left behind?

I thought also of her husband, a careless slip on a wet deck, standing unharnessed near the edge, the concrete of the water coming to meet him as he fell. How long had he treaded water, his veins turning to ice?

What Isaiah didn't know was that I left Floathouse Bay once when he and Birdman were on a walkabout. They did that sometimes, a rifle slung across Birdman's shoulder, a walking staff in his other hand, climbing out of sight into the muskeg and beyond. They only left for a short while, long enough for the morning fog to dissolve. Whatever they talked about, they did not say, but I imagined they went back to the small, humid country where they were young men, metal necklaces burning like fire around their necks.

On one of those days the sereneness of Floathouse Bay was not enough to hold me back. I had been alone with my thoughts too long, the book on tanning hides not enough to keep my attention. The pull of home was too strong. It was easy to forget the bad and remember only the good.

The Lund fired up like magic, and I held onto the tiller, unzipping the water of the bay. Racing the flood tide, the boat moved ten, twenty knots as the bulge of water pushed me out into the strait. My hair flew behind me like a flag, and my eyes watered from the kiss of the salt spray. This was the first time I had been out in the ocean for weeks and its immenseness frightened me at first. Islands with trees like crowded teeth in a stranger's mouth were all that kept me from being the only dot in a field of blue. The fishing fleet was nowhere in sight, holed up somewhere down the coast. A pod of dolphins kept me company instead, playing in my wake.

I had headed north, past all the small cuts in the coast that the *Coast Pilot* had named variations of the same theme. Gods Pocket. Lords Pocket. "God must wear cargo pants," Uncle Dean had joked once, pointing at the chart with a stubby finger, half of it mangled from an accident with kelp in the prop, years ago when he didn't know better. The southern swell rolled mercilessly into those pockets, washing the beaches high into the trees and rolling the same drift-wood logs over and over on the cobbles and off. No place to seek long-term refuge, these were places of last resort where indeed you might pray for deliverance.

I knew this section of coast only from the nautical charts because we never had gone this far south. My father had drawn a line on this section of map, telling us it was dangerous to go farther. Better to stick close to what we knew, he had said. I had studied what lay below the line often, trying to translate the terse words: "Awash at LW" and "Sh" were places to avoid, barely submerged rocks and shoals. Lines of breakers were marked on the charts; places where water slammed into rock shelves with enough force to flip a boat.

There was a whole set of descriptions for the sea floor: rock, mud, sand, or gravel. Numbers marched up and down the page, the depth you had before the bottom came up to meet a boat. Someone had figured all this out once by trial and error. Still, there were wrecks. We had seen them on the beaches, abandoned pilothouses shoved far into the sand by tides, scattered metal rusting across the rocks.

I could study the charts for hours, but the ocean was far from being completely known. Around the shallow edges of each small bay, silver-lined throats of eddies churned, boat-snatchers. Sticky mud filled shallow estuaries. In an open boat, I had to pick the safest line and the charts could not always tell me which one to choose.

As I passed by one of the cargo pockets, the engine cut out with a sigh. The boat bobbed in the swell, pushed toward the sharp rock line. In minutes it could be tossed like driftwood, a hundred pieces washing up on an isolated shore. When I scrambled to pull the starter cord, the engine bumbled along in the way that meant there was water in the fuel. I blamed that for the reason I turned back, that and the dark brow of a storm far out to sea, blowing in my direction. I knew those were not the only reasons.

Maybe Isaiah did know. Maybe he heard the ticking of a cooling engine as he and Birdman strolled back along the bay. Maybe he saw me, my hair slick with saltwater as I hurried to drop back into my chair. But he said nothing about any of those things, only stamping his boots to loosen the mud from the estuary. "Looks like someone could use a hot cup of cowboy coffee," he said heartily. I loved him in that moment, both for what he said and did not say. Pretending to read words blurred on the page, I thought about how little the two men had and how much they had given me.

If I had said that out loud, they would have thought I meant prawns from the pot, eaten half raw, pungent venison fried up in a pan. I knew it was more than that, something intangible, sweet as the unexpected taste of sugar on my lips. I might have called it hope.

Three

When I was ten years old, there was a time when things had been good for the longest I could remember. There were no voices knifing the night, no slammed doors. He had changed, my mother whispered in the kitchen. He had promised that things would always be this way. The days, she said, would melt into each other, smooth and sweet like butter.

It was noon, September. The best month of all. The rain cleared out some of the time, leaving us with days baked crisp, each one a sunny hedge against the winter to come. A good month to forget what had been and what would be. The blueberry bushes had been turning blood red on the avalanche slopes. The days were shortening, entire minutes given over to night. At the estuary, the place where briny water mixed with fresh, the tide fell slowly, reluctantly, the way it always did after midpoint.

My father had set the anchor on the bow of the boat, holding on to one end of the line he had attached to it. Then he shoved the boat hard out into the water. When it was as far as it would go, he yanked on the rope tied to the anchor and it splashed into the sea. He wound the end of the line around a rock far up on the shore, tying it off with a bowline knot.

"They call this an Indian anchor," he told me. "You have to do it right or else you have to swim for the boat later on. Either that or you're high and dry when you get back. You remember what that's like. This isn't a good place to be after dark, either way."

In the river, the salmon were dying as they swam. Driven by an invisible force, they pushed upstream, bumping against my boots with sightless, milky eyes. They pooled in the stagnant eddies, their backs humped, mold growing over them in a fine green film. The bears had been eating them, gulping chunks of belly meat and leaving the rest for the birds.

The bodies of fish lay everywhere, dead and dying, their smell sinking into my clothes and hair. It was a smell that clung to us long after we had scrubbed everything down. It was something we had to just wait out. A raft of red-lipped gulls floated as close as they dared, squabbling over scraps. A dozen eagles perched in the trees, also waiting it out.

"Where are the bears?" I asked.

"Watching us from the woods," my father answered. "Don't you feel them?"

I had shivered a little with terror and delight, looking around. I had imagined that I could feel them, curled up in their day beds just out of sight. I thought that I could smell them too. I knew that bears generally left people alone, but sometimes they did not. Ernie brought us the news of times when they did not. A blueberry picker on the mainland had grappled with a sow briefly in head-high brush. A pair of backpackers on the other side of the island had been scratched on the legs by a bear investigating their tent, pitched unwisely next to a bear highway. It happens, my father always said when Ernie told his stories. He shrugged. Not to us, he said.

We had left the river and walked through the tidal flat, pushing through grass taller than our heads. I lost sight of him once and all I could see was grass moving as if pushed by an invisible wind.

Mud sucked at my boots and I hurried to keep up, taking two steps to his one.

This was not quite sea, not quite land, my father had told me. It was not a place you could count on. Not solid like land, not supple like sea. The best thing to do was to hurry through places like this, he said, the places in between.

At the edge of the tidal flat we paused. We had come to an alder thicket. It grew high up on the avalanche slopes and down through the valley, a solid mass of impenetrable brush.

My father beckoned. "This way," he said, and I followed him into a tunnel that wormed through the alder. The curved passage was just high enough to stand in, just wide enough for our bodies. Over our heads the branches formed a ceiling, a thick woven mat that blocked out the light.

"What is this?" I asked. My father stepped in the same places the bears did, and I copied him, setting my boots carefully in the muddy depressions.

"The bear tunnels," he said. "The bears made these. This is how they get from their day beds to the salmon stream. They've been walking this way for hundreds of years."

I stayed on his heels. Going in felt to me like being swallowed down a bear's throat. It stunk of bears, of decaying fish and something else, a scent I could not name but that only belonged to bears. Icy water dripped off the branches, running under my collar and down my back. The tunnel creaked and groaned as the alders moved in the wind. Anything could be in there. Anything at all.

I did not ask him what would happen if a bear was coming the opposite way. I could only imagine it, a blur of claws and teeth, and I shivered, sticking close to him.

Finally, after what seemed like hours, we had walked out into a giant forest. The spruce trees that grew here were bigger than I had ever seen, their bases fat globes, their tops hundreds of feet into the sky. Moss hung in sodden clumps from the branches, higher than I could climb, thicker around than my father's arms. In some places, masses of plants grew like hair from the trunks, plants my father called epiphytes, plants that feed on only air.

These trees were older than time, he told me. They had been here before any of us were born, before Vancouver sailed past here on his way north. This place was never crushed under the weight of the glaciers like the rest of the island, he said. It had remained ice free, becoming a refuge for the bears, isolating them from their inland cousins. They waited out the ice here, slowly becoming their own species, their fur turning a deeper, darker brown. The bears here were more closely related to polar bears than grizzlies, he said as we walked under the big trees.

It was as dark as evening under the canopy. The rain never reached the ground. Nothing moved, but I could feel the shadows of bears.

"This place belongs to the bears," my father said. His dark eyes shone.

"The first time I found this place, I was seventeen. I had just come to Alaska, come up from California with Dean. Bought an old boat for a song, and we stumbled in here by accident seeking a good place to anchor. We ended up beaching the boat by accident, a pair of rookies, so we had hours to kill before the tide. Let's go walk around, I said, see what there is to see here, and Dean said hell no, but I knew if I went, he had to come too, couldn't show he was afraid. We walked straight across the estuary like you and I just did. We just kept walking, like we were being pulled in. We found the tunnels and dared each other to walk through them. Once we got to this forest I saw ten bears in here eating grass like a herd of cows. We found trees that we could climb and stayed so quiet I didn't even breathe, and we watched their eyes. It got dark while I sat up there, but I didn't want to leave. I wanted to watch them all night. Their eyes were like little campfires in the dark, and we could hear them as they moved through the tall grass. Dean was scared to death. Shook like a willow the whole time, shook the whole tree, even though he tried to hide it from me."

"Weren't you afraid?"

He laughed. "Some," he said. "It was crazy not to be afraid. But nobody ever goes back here. The *Coast Pilot* warns against it. Too narrow, too sandy to hold an anchor. Nobody even knows these trees are here. The bears guard this place. We have a truce here, the bears and me. An understanding. They protect the trees, I protect them."

It hadn't really made sense at the time. Bears could travel hundreds of miles. My schoolbooks had told me so. The bears here in Enchantment Bay could be the bears his clients shot several bays down the coast. But looking at my father, I had known he truly believed in what he was saying. Because he believed it, I had decided to believe it too.

Now I wondered if everything I had believed was untrue. My father had always said that the bears were our bread and butter. The bears were the reason we could stay here. Nobody could stay here without killing, he had said. Killing was necessary. "I wouldn't survive living anywhere else," he had told us. "And you won't either. Think you would like living in an apartment building listening to strangers breathe?"

Birdman and Isaiah lived here without killing bears. Instead they bent over the grass flats, painstakingly pulling the tips of fiddleheads and boiling up a fishy-smelling green stew. They collected beach pea, nori algae, and sea lettuce. They filled up bowls with salmonberries. They trapped, but only in small numbers to supplement their disability checks. Birdman hunted for deer, but one animal could sustain them for months.

I studied them as they moved from floathouse dock to boat, from boat to land, one elastic limbed and giant, the other short and elfin. Isaiah and Birdman reminded me of the way water squirmed through layers of stone, probing for weakness. They blended into the country in a way my father never had. For the first time I realized that I could slip inside the skin of a place without tearing it open.

Four

Isaiah and I took a breather in the muskeg, working the traps, our feet sinking deeper as though we were growing there. He picked up our conversation from a few days ago as if it had been just minutes. "You aren't the first of your family to live here. The three of them stayed here," he said. "Althea, Roy, and Dean. Did you know that? Dean and Roy first, for a couple of years, and then the three of them after she came. It was the last winter they were all together, the winter before Dean up and moved to town. Boy howdy, we lit up this bay, us and the Hudson boys."

My mother had lived here? I had seen no signs of her. The floathouse brimmed with things others had left behind and which Isaiah insisted on storing in case they came back. Besides Honey's clothes, a chalky white whale's pelvis gathered green mold in the corner of the outhouse. A mask someone had brought back from India and abandoned hung askew in the front room. Even an entire mink coat, ragged from mice's meals, lay puffy and sodden with humidity in the mud room. These were all things that had meant something to somebody at one time. I had not thought to look for souvenirs of my family.

"I didn't know," I said. "They never told me."

My father had always told me that going to Floathouse Bay meant entering a boiling pot of crazy. The people there were twisted by the war, he said, knotted up like a rope gone bad from too much saltwater and wind. Friends once, he had said, but no more. He never said why, and I had always known not to ask. Something dark lurked there, something impossible to breach.

"What were they like when they were young?" I asked. "What was it like, that last summer and the winter after that?"

Isaiah lit up his wooden pipe, inhaling deeply. "It was like dodging lighting, being around those two boys," he said. "Stop your heart or make you high, one. Dean and Roy, they were electric together. One would dare the other to jump bare ass into that cold water, nothing between them and the Lord but a smile. Climb the red cliffs without a rope. Sleep when you're dead, Roy used to say. There was always competition between them. Had been since they were boys, I gathered. Their father favored Dean, and Roy kept trying to prove he was as good. You could feel it when you were around the two of them, but still, that summer, until she came, was the best I've ever had."

"What do you mean, until she came?"

"Ah," Isaiah said. "Let me paint you a picture of that summer. I think of it often. It was scary dry, hardly rained at all, and you know how we catch the clouds on this side of the island. No frog stranglers that summer, hardly a drop. Blue skies every day, and it seemed like all of our plans were going to work out. But Roy got restless, took off on the barge for town and the Hell and Gone, to stir up some trouble, he said. He wasn't one for quiet. It made him too nervous just sitting with his thoughts, he said. Life was too damn long to be sweet and innocent, he said. He was gone two weeks and when he came back, she was with him."

"Where did he find her?" I asked, remembering the story my mother had told me, a sweet story, a tale I had always thought might end up being something like my own love story someday.

"The Hell and Gone, that bar in town, is where you find the losers and the drifters and the people who need saving. All of the people who come to Alaska thinking they can turn into someone else, leave the old person behind. It doesn't work that way, a lot of us have learned. Whatever you're looking for here, you might as well bring it with you, because you're going to be the same damn soul you were when you hopped on that ferry in Bellingham."

His eyes went far away the way they did sometimes, and I knew he was talking about more than just my mother and father.

"When Roy found Althea at the Hell and Gone across the island and brought her here, it changed everything," Isaiah said finally. "You could feel it, a cut to the air. Like winter coming.

"The story she gave us was that she came to Alaska following a no-good asshat who left her with no cash and no place to go. That's when the trouble started. Both of the boys, so in love with her that they did crazy things to try to get her attention. Cannonballing off cliffs in the dark. Walking up salmon streams thick with bears, no flashlight. In the end she chose Roy. Dean, he was so used to winning, didn't know how to lose. 'My brother, the golden boy,' Roy used to call him. Roy always thought he never measured up to Dean. This time he had, and he let Dean know it."

He stowed his pipe and picked up his share of the traps. A cough began deep in his belly and worked its way out through the length of his body. Finally he spat out a glob of phlegm onto the ground. "Dean was the best damn pilot in southeast Alaska, at least that was the word up and down the coast. He would land where none of the other pilots would even spit out the window. Flew like a guy with nothing to lose. I can't help but think that she put some kind of wrench to his heart. Half the time he flew like he didn't care if he would make it back."

The story did not fit. "My father said Dean went through women like Kleenex," I recalled. "Living in town, he had his pick of all of those girls working the slime line."

Isaiah shrugged. "Don't know about cannery girls. Just know what I saw. I know that nothing fazed him. It could be the crappiest day out there, fog down to the deck, and he would fly anyway. 'Just about took the mast off a sailboat, I was flying so low,' he used to say. And laugh about it. We all waited for that day, the one when he never showed back up at the float dock."

A silence as thick as fog spread between us. Most of us never spoke much of the dead; they were too much of a reminder of the thin line we all walked. Here, there were no safety nets like you had in the Lower 48, my father used to like to say. Talking about the people who had never made it back brought us too close to that edge. Here, my father had said, you made your own luck.

"One thing he said, the last day," I told Isaiah, remembering. "We had a topographic map out for some reason, maybe because there were some clients hanging around asking about what it was like above the bay. My uncle pointed at a little lake and told us that if he never came back, that was where we should look for him. Lake of the Fallen Moon, it was called. He said that he would be kicking back in the blueberry patch. No clients with a million duffels, no fighting the weather in a piece of flimsy aluminum with floats. Living the dream, he said. Then he took off into the storm and we never saw him again."

"Lake of the Fallen Moon. Pretty name. They looked there, didn't they? The Civil Air Patrol, Search and Rescue?"

"They looked everywhere." Uncle Dean had just vanished as if he had never been.

A pair of does that had been bedded down jumped up on legs as slender as pencils and bounded away from us as Isaiah and I began to walk. A few steps into the muskeg and they stopped to look, freezing into place as though, motionless, they could not be seen. I watched them, so sure of their invisibility.

I was not sure of anything, even the spongy ground beneath my boots. The past felt as murky and bottomless as the sinkholes we skirted. At the same time it dawned on me that there in Isaiah's memory could be the answers to the puzzle that was Never Summer Bay. If I could learn enough, I could figure out where to go next from Floathouse Bay.

"The trouble, you said," I reminded Isaiah. "What trouble?"

"Oh, the trouble," he answered. "Well, I've got to tell you some backstory. How much of this do you know? Nothing? Roy and Dean showed up a couple years after we did. People were just starting to come to the coast then. Hippies, runaways, strays of all kinds. Birdman and I had bribed Ernie with a few dollars to tow this old floathouse into a bay where we wouldn't be run out right away. We were scraping away at things, not really making much of a go at it. Ernie told Roy and Dean to look us up, that there were a couple of vets living rough out there who might be able to teach them a thing or two."

The wind shifted imperceptibly, carrying the scent of something only the deer could smell. They dashed away from us and slipped into the valley beyond.

Isaiah watched the deer run long past where I could see them, shading a hand over his eyes. "Fat ones. Good eating," he said. "Dean and Roy being out here, it felt like Birdman and I weren't as alone. Between the two of them, they scratched up enough money to buy the private chunk of ground in Never Summer. Land went for pennies then, not like now. They lived here though, on the sailboat, while they drew up the plans and got the materials. It was going to be their place, and they seemed to agree on something for once. A dozen guys had tried it and gave up, driven out by the rain and the gales. I knew I had to stick it out. This was the end of the line for Birdman and me. I wasn't so sure about the boys. Roy seemed to think he could bully his way in to the country, make it adapt to him rather than the other way around. I tried to tell him different, but he never listened. My way or the highway, he said. He's just that kind of man.'"

He motioned for a nail. "After they came, we hatched up this plan to trap some, share a greenhouse, sell some vegetables to the store in town. Dean would do the milk run for the rest of the folks living out here, he just had to get certified on floats, already had his pilot's license from down south. Birdman and I got checks from Uncle Sam, we would get by. Ernie was in on it, he got his cut when we bought supplies from him. But once Althea showed up, Roy decided that Dean was out. Didn't want him around her, he said, Dean wanted to steal her away from him. He was flat convinced. Roy said that Dean could still bring in the clients, but he couldn't live there. It would be him and her living there, just them, nobody else, and he would get a broker, advertise in hunting magazines. Bring in rich men from Outside to hunt bears. Once he started up, he made it look easy, and a hundred other guys thought they could do it too. Southeast was full of guys who didn't know a thing about this place and didn't care neither."

He sighed. "Didn't feel right to me. Eat what you kill, I told him, and the bears are our grandfathers, we need them more than they need us. Roy might have liked bears well enough, but he was always out for himself. Said there were plenty of bears as long as he chose the right ones. We almost came to blows over it, except I don't fight anymore. Instead we split the coast in two. Birdman and I would stay south, and he would stay north."

I didn't understand how you could love a thing and still hurt it, and I told Isaiah so. "How do you mean?" he asked.

He hunched down on his heels, nails rimming his mouth, and listened as if he had all the time in the world. That was one of the things I liked about him. He gave a person time to come up with words, to make sense of the thoughts wrestling in her head.

Finishing up with the last trap, we worked our way down country, heading for the sea. Clear plates of ice lined the stream we were following. Only the busy movement of the water kept it from freezing entirely. Soon even that would not be enough and this stream would be encased in a solid cocoon. The water that I scooped into my canteen came with shards of ice that slid down my throat, making my head throb. Fingers of frost lay etched on the meadow, winter's breath on the landscape.

Our feet crunched in the grass. "If he loved her so much, why did he hurt her?" I asked finally. "She forgave him, every time."

Looking back, I could see where we had been, patches of green in the white, Isaiah's feet turning out wide in his duct-taped boots, my tracks marching small and determined beside his. "Ah, Winnie," Isaiah said. "I've lived a long time, and I still don't have all the answers. I just know that something is broken in Roy. Maybe it was trying to step out of Dean's shadow, maybe it was something else, but together, both of them, Althea and Roy, are like oil and fire. They stir something up in each other that's best left alone. They should never have met in the first place." He glanced at me. "But then there wouldn't be you. So there is that one good thing."

A small smile spread across my face and I ducked my head. "I mean it, girl," he said. "When you drove in here, I turned to Birdman and said, that's their daughter. I knew it right off. Her silver hair and his courage, driving that boat alone in that big ocean. I want no part of this, I told Birdman. She's on the next barge out of here. But he said, just give her a chance. This surprised me, it being Birdman. He doesn't trust anybody. But now I see that you're the best parts of both of them. His spark and her sweet."

We had come out onto the shore, and the stew of kelp and fish filled my lungs. "Spin the dial with Roy and you either landed on brilliant or crazy," he continued. "Never knew which one to expect. That's what made it a hard go. Loved the brilliant, hated the crazy. Althea, well, she never said much about her past. She'd clam up when you asked her, mouth like she was sucking on lemons. All I gathered was that she came from someplace in Ohio, Indiana, one of those flyover states, never fit in with her parents' plans for her, and then she followed a man to Alaska, one of those types that promises the world and then leaves you behind when he chances on something better. The only time I saw her crack, one night when we all got into the whiskey pretty heavy, was when she said, 'Any story I tell you would be better than my real life.' Then she shut right up and acted like she had never said a word."

I thought about all the stories my mother had given me. Whales singing the same song through the ocean. James Tucker, dead of some misfortunate that changed every time we went to his grave. She had spun a story of our lives too, but she had left out the weak parts. "She told me that she met him on the barge in a storm. Both of them nomads, looking for a better life. He held her hand while the boat wallowed in the troughs below a steep sea. That it was meant to be, like a fairytale. By the time they reached Never Summer Bay they knew they would be together forever. That's what she told me. And I believed it." I felt the sting of betrayal. She had not trusted me with the truth.

"That must have been how she wanted it to have been," Isaiah said. "Plenty of people living on this coast under the names they weren't born with. Plenty of people with different stories than the ones they lived. Noses so high in the air they would drown in a rainstorm, as if they never did anybody wrong. Who is ever going to know different if stories don't match up?"

We walked the shoreline, our feet slipping in the kelp and rocks. Somewhere above us a floatplane droned, moving in and out of the clouds, en route to the fish weir or the field camp.

"I can guess what it was like in Never Summer," Isaiah said. He looked troubled. "Roy was always a quick trigger. The man could start an argument in an empty house, but it seemed to get worse after she came. Birdman and I should have done something sooner, but what could we do? We let the years slip by, tucked up in this bay.

We knew if we left it things would change. We've got old bones and we thought we deserved a little peace."

I thought about the way they lived, barely denting the bay, not cutting or burning or building the way my family had. If they ever left, the floathouse would eventually tumble into the sea. The greenhouse would collapse into a pile of old boards. There would be no trace of them left behind. Isaiah was right: they deserved peace.

We dropped the traps we hadn't used in a clatter on the dock. Back in the floathouse, the ropes strained and creaked at their moorings. Candles flickered like passing thoughts. We sat like old people in our chairs, watching the night.

In Floathouse Bay there were hours and hours to think, unlike where I had come from. In Never Summer the tasks piled up. There was wavering under the weight of the fully loaded cart, bringing shotguns in their yellow dry bags and boxes of food and camouflage gear down to the boat while the clients watched, not helping. There were the freshwater tanks to fill and fuel to pump from the barrels. There were the wives, who sometimes stayed behind, who we had to placate with fat-free muffins and Jane Fonda videos. Only when the clients left and the rooms were clean was there time to think about something other than if there was enough hot water for the wives' endless showers, how their blow dryers were draining the solar, and if the men would go home puffed up with importance and a glossy brown hide.

In Floathouse Bay I had time to think about years and love and how one changed the other. "Were you ever married?" I asked. "Either of you?"

"Sure," Isaiah said. "Just never took. Always wanted a woman as sweet as young fiddleheads but ended up with the bitter. And Birdman had three successful marriages, didn't you, buddy?"

Birdman nodded without moving his eyes from the book he was holding. He had a daughter somewhere in the world, a girl my age with cinnamon hair. He kept a picture of her hanging in the greenhouse, its edges warped by the humid air. She was long gone, vanished into some corn-fed state down south, Isaiah had told me, taken away by one of the women Birdman had once loved.

"Someday you are going to have someone who will hang on you like a Christmas ornament," Isaiah said. "Believe it."

I wanted to believe it. I had only read about the starburst of fear and longing as a boy leaned in for a first kiss. But the only boys I knew about on our coast lived at the fish weir, separated from me by miles of open water. I heard their squeaky voices sometimes on the radiophone, half men, half children, but we had never met. I had once dreamed about Sam, but now I wondered if the look in his eyes had been the same as what I saw in Isaiah's. I feared that I had mistaken Sam's kindness for something deeper.

"What happened?" I asked, and what I really meant was this: how do people change? How had the boys my uncle and father had been, skin bronzed by summer, two laughing daredevils, turned into the two men I had known later in their lives? Those men had been like this: one who was always leaving us wanting more as he hopped on his plane with a wave and the other an uneasy mixture of sun and rain.

I had watched tightly woven kelp rafts outside our bay slowly dissolve, the driftwood and opaque Japanese fishing floats captured within suddenly set free to bash upon the red cliffs. Were people the same, their tiny cracks widening without realizing until it was too late, until they were different people entirely? Could you ever go back to the way you had been?

"Never loved anyone as much as I loved being out alone in the wilderness," Birdman said.

Birdman rarely spoke. When he did, it was with a rasp of rusty hinges. He rolled words around in his mouth like marbles before letting them go. In the war, Isaiah told me, he had been the one their platoon had counted on to cut sign. Cutting sign, he said, was finding and determining who or what had passed. Birdman could tell everything about you from the way your feet pressed into wet sand, Isaiah said. What you carried, if you were in a hurry, even what was on your mind. That was why Birdman did all the hunting. When I asked if I could go, Birdman nodded. "Free country," he said.

Five

All along the coast, cedar trees were dying. They had been dying for as long as I could remember. One summer when I was eight, without any warning, two scientists had chartered a plane and flown into Never Summer Bay, their packs bristling with tubes and measuring sticks.

"We're here to study cedar decline," the older one said loudly when my father rushed to meet them at the dock. When he heard the plane, he warned me to stay back, but I followed him anyway, zigzagging down the dock from the pile of crab pots to the boat shed, strangers who weren't clients an unusual occurrence in our bay. To me it was worth the risk of being discovered.

"This is private property," my father said. His face flushed red, a danger sign that I knew well. It wasn't directed at me, so I stayed put. "You can't come ashore here."

The man adjusted his glasses and cleared his throat while, safe next to the plane, the younger one with the soul patch and clamshell necklace rolled his eyes. "I know that, sir, we have maps. But the national forest starts about a mile back from here. We thought we'd just pass through. The Forest Service told us we could."

"Fellows, you thought wrong."

The young curly haired one had gathered his courage and stepped forward. "But this is the best example of cedar decline on the island.

Don't you want to know why this is happening?" He looked right at me, blowing my cover from where I peeked out from behind the boat shed. "I bet you study this in school, little girl. It could be that the winters are getting warmer because of climate change and the roots aren't insulated like they used to be. Or it could be something else. Nobody knows. We have a grant from a university."

My father lifted his right hand, until now hidden behind his back. In it he held his .375 H&H rifle by the stock. He aimed it near their feet. "Private property," he repeated. "Winnie, go back to the house. Now."

Disobeying, I silently crept farther behind the boat shed, unable to stop watching. My mother was suddenly there too, clasping my hand.

The scientists started to cinch on their packs.

My father lifted the rifle higher. He worked the action. "Private property," he repeated.

Inside the plane the chubby pilot dropped his newspaper. "Jesus!" he gasped. "I told you guys this would happen!" He fired up the prop. The scientists scrambled aboard in a jumble of arms and legs. Without waiting for them to fasten their belts, the pilot step-taxied to the end of the bay and took off. Their wake rolled across the water and slurped against the pilings.

All three of us stood together at the end of the dock. Looking up I saw their faces pressed like moons against the windows. After the sound of the plane faded, the fight went out of him like it always did, a blaze of fierce white anger that burned itself out the way my campfires did when I did not wait long enough before piling on bigger, wetter logs.

"There used to be a herring run here, girls," he said. "The water looked like milk for miles. Herring spawn. You could throw in a spruce branch like the Tlingit did and pick it out a day later covered with herring eggs. Salty. Delicious. And what happened? Fished out. Just like the halibut. Gone. And just skiff on up to Josephine Island

and you can see the clear-cuts, all those big trees, sent on to Japan."
He deflated, collapsing on the bench, his head in his hands. His
voice was muffled, as though he was on the edge of tears, though
I knew that was not possible. "They take and take from this place
and don't give anything back. I've watched them take the trees. I've
watched them take the fish. I've watched them blast the rocks,
looking for gold. I won't let it happen here."

Not understanding, I piped up. "But you bring bear hunters here.
What's the difference?" Behind his back, my mother shook her head,
a warning. But my father's mood had shifted already; it was safe.
He smiled and sat up, running his fingers through my tangled hair.
"You're a smart girl, Winnie. But listen. I never let them shoot the
sows, or the grandfather bears, the ones that are almost nocturnal.
And I'll tell you something. They haunt me, the bears. You wait, one
day my ship will come in, and I'll get out of the bear killing business.
I've had about enough of killing."

He never said which ship that would be. For a long time, I thought
that he meant a real ship, and I spent hours sitting on Lookout Point
scanning the horizon for it. I had pictured it as a sailboat gliding in
to the bay without a sound to pick him up and carry him away from
us. I both wanted this and feared it.

It had been the same way for me with the bears. I hated the
swaggering with the skins, the rest of the bear tossed out into the
deep woods like trash. Bear hunting paid for our roof, my mother
used to tell me, though I thought I saw the same dislike in her eyes.
Do you want to end up in Floathouse Bay, with nothing, my father
had added, not a question but a statement. We had to be neutral,
not let it get to us, my mother told me, but she got up with her plate
and went to the kitchen when the stories got too loud.

There were ghost forests in Floathouse Bay too. Birdman passed
through them without comment even when the wind ran through

them, making them sing. We walked single file, separately but within sight, leaning over slightly from the weight of our rain-soaked packs. Climbing above the bay, we headed east through a scattering of trees. The body of the land changed under our feet, a long slow sweep of amber belly and smooth rock taking over from the muskeg.

Following Birdman, I walked through a basin scooped out by glaciers thousands of years ago. Mountains shouldered in on all sides, their steep granite walls blocking out all but a sliver of the sky. If it ever stopped raining long enough for the sun to show its face, light would only fall here for a few hours before it disappeared again for the night.

An unhurried river full of glacial melt, the color of white chalk, wound through the valley floor, sprawling in long, lazy circles among the scattered hemlocks and alder. Above, a ragged hem of clouds clamped down tight, enclosing us in a cup of rain and fog.

The walking was easier here. The river was lined with fat gravel bars made up of stones tumbled down from far up in the headwaters during the snowmelt, when I imagined that this valley must erupt in an ecstatic torrent of water and sound. Slowly the river was turning the rocks into sand. The rocks were polished from wind and rain, each one a smooth, perfect round ball.

Sometimes we had to leave the river and travel on the side slopes when the banks became tangled with logs. In Birdman's wake, I plodded up through low blueberry shrubs, the berries long since withered or eaten by bears. When we could, we left the cedars to their secrets and dropped back down to the river.

There were stories in the sand if you knew how to read them. Birdman stopped to point out the animal highways. Here, the smooth hollow where a family of river otters had slid down the bank from the trees to the water. There, where an eagle had landed and captured something small and vulnerable, pockmarking the mud with its talons. There were no tracks he could not name.

I looked back at our footprints, two wavering lines stretching back behind us. How long before the rain erased the tracks as if we had never passed through here? I shook in my damp clothes, imagining that we could be erased as easily, the country swallowing us up in one big gulp. Hypothermia. Drowning. Bears.

We had been following a pair of bears. Birdman silently pointed out where their tracks crossed the bar here, a mother and a cub bound for the promise of still ripe blueberries farther up the valley. Their prints were sunk deep into the wet ground. The bears had crossed only hours earlier; sand had not begun to cave in their tracks.

I spoke in a low voice. "Late for them to be this high, isn't it? Not much to eat up here. Plenty of salmon down below."

"Some females never come down from the high country," Birdman said. He didn't say why, but I knew. The females lingered on because it was safer here. Even though there were salmon below—rich, savory food they desperately needed before the coming winter—there was danger too. Here they could hide their cubs deep in the valley and protect them from the boars who might kill them. It was a risk: stay safe and gamble on the fickle blueberry crop or venture lower and become prey.

Looking at the prints, I realized that I had almost forgotten why I was still in Floathouse Bay. It seemed to me that I had been living here forever, that this was my life now. That there was no real destination, that I might walk through valleys like this year after year with a silent man and a rifle. That I was not a body anymore but only motion, like rivers, like wind, flowing through an unknown country.

Birdman stopped for a reason only he knew. "Here," he said, motioning for me to stand back to back with him. I knew why. He was hunting deer in the most dangerous way possible. He would blow a call designed to sound like a fawn in trouble. It would draw the deer, but it could also draw a hungry bear. Hunters had been killed that way, a bear creeping up behind an unprotected back. That was why I faced the opposite direction, to look for bears.

My father had never hunted that way. It was impossible, he said. The clients were full to the brim with bluff and swagger, barely covering up their fear with gold chains and big rings and a strut that dared anyone to question them. After they left, my father would share stories with us about the man who collapsed in a heap in the muskeg, claiming exhaustion, the temper tantrums, the fear of high places. It was better for them to see the bears coming, to lie in wait in the hush of a forest. To have the upper hand. Otherwise they would cut and run.

I pressed my shoulders against Birdman's back, watching. Nothing moved but the river. The deer were all waiting out the rain under the trees, invisible.

A raw wind picked up, a down-canyon breeze, coming from somewhere we had yet to reach. As it passed through the dead trees, they rattled with a mournful wail. A whole forest was gone on these hillsides. The wood was so strong and tough that the snags would stand for years.

Where would we all be when the trees tumbled down? Birdman was old, his body winnowed down to muscle and bone. White hair poked out of the ball cap he always wore, and he walked with an old hurt in his leg. How much longer would he be alive, him and Isaiah both? Where would I go from here if I lost them? I felt lonely pressed against his back, as if I had no home anywhere.

I heard him clear his throat as I wiped unwanted tears away with a mitten. "Three kinds of tide," he said. "Slack, flood, low. Which one are you?"

It felt like a test and I wanted to get the answer right. My father, of course, was most like the high tide. Without apology it swept in to claim the beach, shrinking it by fifteen feet in hours. You could lose everything in the high tide, and our family had, mistakenly pitching the tent in the sedges, carelessly leaving guns out, or building our warming fire low enough to be swallowed. The high tide was a bully, tossing driftwood far into the beach fringe, gulping up the rocks and drowning everything in its path. If you turned your back on the high tide, you would regret it. At the same time the high tide was a magnificent floating carpet, bringing us treasures from the sea. Rafts of bulbous amber-colored bull kelp rode it and so did plastic bottles with Asian characters. It spit up sand dollars and pink-throated shells. Sometimes it brought us nothing. You just never knew with the high tide.

I saw my mother in the way the low tide moved: gentle, reluctant, creeping away like it did not want to be noticed, gradually letting go of its hold on the land. It was easy to discount the low tide as inconsequential. But there was another side to the ebb. It could fool you into complacency like leaving a skiff high and dry because you thought there was plenty of time to anchor, or if the person left with the boat didn't push it out into deeper water fast enough. If I stepped in the wrong place in the tide flats, the sticky mud would set up like concrete until I had to abandon my boots and crawl to safer ground. Years ago Ernie had told us that a woman died near Anchorage in Turnagain Arm when she got mired in the flats, rescuers finally giving up and handing her a straw to breathe through as the tide moved back in.

Because I didn't want to be like either of them, that left me with slack tide, the last of the three. Slack was the bridge between the two extremes, a suspension, a holding of breath. Slack made it possible to go places I never could at any other time. During slack I could navigate by kayak through the slinky steep-walled passage into Floathouse Bay. If I had tried that during any other tide I would be hurled out of my boat as the water poured in or out of the constricted channel. You wanted to round the points of the bays during slack because ebb or flow turned it into a washing machine. In contrast, I knew that you could let down your guard a little with slack, leave your boats untied, float. I was fine with slack.

I felt Birdman's body give a little. "Nothing wrong with slack tide," he said. "I'm partial to it myself. I ask everyone who comes here that question. Tells you a lot about a person, the answer they give."

He shouldered his rifle. "Deer are shy today. Come on. Want to show you something." I followed him as we walked out of the valley and into the forest.

Ancient spruce trees surrounded us, their fluted, shaggy bases larger around than the two of us could reach. Wide legged at their bases, they spiraled upward to become thick-bodied giants.

The forest floor was soft and yielding. Under our feet ferns fanned over the ground in a continuous feathery green plate. Sprinkled among them, the devil's club shot upward, their stalks full of vicious spines. Skunk cabbage unfurled its thickly veined leaves. Birdman touched one of the trees reverently. "Spiky needles to protect the tree from evil thoughts, the Tlingit said."

We lay on our backs for a while in the moss. In the gloom the trees cast it could have been midnight or midafternoon. This was a place of perpetual shadow, the canopy entwined far overhead in a dense mat.

It was a kind of vertigo, lying on my back gazing upward. It seemed to me that I was in motion instead of the trees, that the ground I was lying on was a ship moving along the ragged edge of the afternoon. The old trees made their own music, creaking deep in their bones, pulling water from the depths of the soil up the length of their trunks. The trees breathed out the same water far above me in cloudy breaths, water that evaporated into the atmosphere and came back down as the light touch of rain. The rain that reached the ground here soaked into the cake-like soil, pooling under the roots of the trees. A tree could drink the same water over and over again for centuries, Birdman said. They would outlast us, he said.

The trees reminded me of the ones in Enchantment Bay. These were distant cousins, perhaps beginning their lives at the same time, sinking their roots deep in duff, that loamy mixture of seeds and dirt and decaying things that could pile up as high as my father was tall.

I wondered where my father was now. The hunts were over, the boats stowed until spring. Sam would have left on the last plane out like he always did, promising to return come spring. Winter meant a slower pace, though there were still tasks to complete. It was when we cleaned rifles, rebuilt engines, and steeled ourselves for the darkness ahead. I pictured my mother and father moving through dim hallways without me, the rhythm of their days unchanging until the manic days of spring.

"She chose him over me," I said, although I had not meant to say it. "How could she choose him?"

Birdman hauled himself upright, wincing slightly. He wrapped a piece of sedge around his fingers and studied it.

"Some people need the sizzle," he said after a time. "Plain old life just isn't enough for them."

I probed the thought like a sore tooth. If he was right, my father was the same way. He took the boat out in twenty-foot seas just to see if he could outrun the weather. Our orange survival suits lay on the bunks below, unworn, because to put them on meant surrender.

"I like the flat lines," Birdman said, and I knew he was thinking of traveling as a young man through a far-off country not long before I was born. I knew from the little Isaiah told me that he and Birdman were the only ones to survive an ambush, lying flat and breathless under the bodies of their dead comrades. I knew that was why he and Isaiah were tied to Floathouse Bay and each other with a knot impossible to unravel. From the time they had been lifted out of the swamp, covered in the blood and brains of their friends, they had made a pact to watch each other's backs. Who else could understand, Isaiah had told me. Others had tried, women, leaning in with looks of concern rippling their faces. But unless you were there, Isaiah said, to smell it and taste it and feel it, you didn't get it, not at all.

I guessed that I liked flat lines too, and I told Birdman so. He reached out a hand to help me up. "You fit right in here with us, then," he said, and I knew I had passed the test.

At night Birdman read books by the kerosene lamp, bifocals perched on his nose. He knew just about everything I could think of to ask: How to cross a river, swollen and chalky from snowmelt. How to spot the places a glacier had been by the rocks and debris it had chewed up on its retreat. The story of the Kiksadi Tlingit survival march across the island after the bloody battles with Russian forces. *We will return to our homeland when the time is right*, the words sending a shiver down my spine. After a time he would stop talking and go away somewhere in his mind. I could see it coming, just like a fog bank over the ocean before it rolled in waves of suffocating cotton over the land.

"Where does he go?" I asked Isaiah one day. We pulled crab pots from the bay, hauling up the rope by hand. It took both of us tugging to bring the dripping pots from deep in the ocean. We sorted through the keepers, throwing the rest back and watching them sink, spread eagled, into the deep blue depths.

Isaiah reached into a bucket of salmon heads and tied two into the pot. He palmed a pair of orange rubber gloves. "Ready?"

I nodded and grasped one end of the pot. Together we heaved it over the side where it fell, slowly turning until I could not see it anymore. All that was left was our red-and-white buoy marking the spot.

Just when I thought that Isaiah had forgotten my question, he leaned his chin on the oar and spoke. "He goes back to the good times, I think," he said. "Maybe back to when he was a kid, barefoot in the long grass, sun shining like it would never quit, before he knew different. He hasn't had an easy go, and I try to make it as simple for him here as I can. You know that we are squatters here, right?" At my nod he went on. "The coast is long and stormy and the government has better things to do than to chase two old men. At least that's what I choose to believe."

I could imagine what would happen to them if they were forced to go. On the few trips to town my father allowed, I had seen men like them through the greasy glass of the Hell and Gone, lined up and leaning sideways on bar stools like kelp in the tide. Smoke lay like a thick membrane over the dim interior. Their eyes, when they met mine through the window, were full of desperate hope. I never wanted that to happen to Isaiah and Birdman. They belonged out here. They were part of this place. I wanted to learn their secrets. I wanted to be just like they were, calm and unhurried, glowing with rain that fell off their jackets and beards, the taste of freedom on their lips.

Six

Just as spring began to loosen winter's grip, sneaking past it on cat feet, just when the sedges in the estuary turned green overnight, the bay itself losing its last layer of ice, Isaiah returned from outside where he always met the barge. He held a piece of paper with writing on it as familiar as my own. His mouth was set in a grim line.

"Trouble up the coast," he said.

I had learned long ago that lives changed in simple ways. A trickle of water from the sky becomes a torrent, a puff of breeze, a gale. A man falls from the sky and is gone forever, the skin of his airplane collapsing into land or sea. Like the games of chess that the clients played when weather pinned them down in the lodge, one tiny move could mean disaster. "Who is gone?" I asked.

"He's alive," Isaiah told me. I didn't have to ask who he meant. He sank into the scarred leather armchair, his face deep in midafternoon shadow. "Got jumped by a bear in Enchantment Bay, but he lived."

Our uneasy truce with the bears had been broken. I had always thought that the bears tolerated us because they knew what was in our hearts. *Bread and butter.* We took their highways, our feet sinking deep in the moss where generations of bears had passed, each stepping in the same places. We fished the same streams, dipping our nets beneath the waterfall to catch sockeye as they jumped skyward. We hunted the same valleys, filling our buckets with blueberries that tasted like sunshine. Even though we heard the stories of the unlucky, it was easy to believe that we were somehow special and that the rules did not apply to us.

I struggled to make sense of it. It was hunting season again, early spring, when the bears emerged ravenous from their dens. They scoured the avalanche chutes for early green-up and wandered the estuaries, easy targets. Bears were everywhere, grouchy from lack of food. It was when we had to be the most careful of all.

"Enchantment Bay? But he didn't hunt the bear tunnels. He wouldn't, even though the biggest bears lived there. He told me so."

"He never would," Isaiah agreed.

"So why was he there? How badly is he hurt?" And what mistake did he make, I wondered, because for this to happen, something must have gone wrong. There had been a blunder, some misstep, even though it was impossible to imagine. A client, missing a shot? That happened all the time. That was why Sam was there with the backup rifle, to take the killing shot. But in Enchantment Bay? Never in Enchantment Bay.

Isaiah wrenched his boots off his feet and moved them close to the woodstove. He took his time about it, carefully positioning first one, and then the other. He regarded them for a moment and then moved them again.

"Ernie said something about a timber sale in that bay," he said finally. "Cruisers were in there, something like that." He glanced at Birdman and some spark flew between them, some old understanding forged by years of friendship.

"Tell me everything," I said. I still could not believe it. My father had been more like a bear than anyone. He stepped in their steps, sometimes even slept in their beds for quick naps. He sat for hours with binoculars trained on bears as they splashed in the salmon streams. He could not have been surprised by a bear. And the trees, what if the loggers took all the trees? The tunnels would disappear, dredged and filled in to make a landing for the barge. The clear waters of the river would be muddied by boat engines. The salmon would circle, confused by the changes to their map. Loggers would swarm like ants, taking out every tree marked with light blue cruiser's paint.

The bay would be scalped like I had seen in the woods near town, lighter patches of impenetrable alder taking the place of ancient trees. It would take more lifetimes than we had in us for the big trees to come back.

Ernie had cataloged all the details and relayed them to Isaiah with the grim amusement of the bored. Mangled leg, face scored by claws. I knew there had to be things he did not see that the bear had left behind: Anger. Disappointment. Betrayal.

"Ernie didn't know anything else, and he won't be back this way for a month, maybe longer. The trees may all be cut by then."

"Maybe they have enough trees," I said. How many could they need? There were so many, enough to build a million houses.

"They never have enough," Birdman said.

"Want to go back there?" Isaiah asked. "We'll make the old flat-bottom boat go if we have to, if that's what it takes."

I shook my head, and they let me go to my room. I could hear them talking as I sat there watching the rain streak the windows. I could not go back there despite what had happened, and Isaiah and Birdman knew it. They had escaped old selves too. They both had tales of ill-fitting lives they had shrugged on like too-small coats after the war. Everyone back home was still the same, they said, while they had irretrievably changed. Alaska, they said, was where you went when there was no other place left to go. Don't ever go back, they said, forgetting their promises. Once you leave, make it for good.

I thought about my father on many nights after that. Not the man who had stormed through the lodge, blazing with a fire I could not only see but feel, a man who could burn us, but the man who had taken me to Enchantment Bay the year I was ten. That memory was almost enough to make me go back. I lay in the single bed where another woman had once dreamed, her wet face in a sagging pillow, listening to the creak of ropes as the floathouse strained against the tide. Some of Honey's sadness seemed to stick to the plywood walls, and it was at night that I most often thought about Never Summer Bay.

I read my mother's letter over and over, trying to understand it. It was like a swift river of words without any shallow place to catch a breath.

Dear Winnie:

I write to you from the place you left. Do you remember it? Are you ever coming back, do you think of us in this bay? Nothing here is the same. Nothing here has been the same for a long, long time. It all began to change the day your father went up the coast to Enchantment Bay. The forest has swallowed him up in its big teeth. By now you have heard the story and what happened to him.

I do not know this gray-faced ghost, who needs his sheets changed from his night sweats, who wakes screaming, who needs me so much. He whines, he sobs, he clings to me. His gnarled hands, grasping at me, pulling, insisting. Juice, water, hot tea, this is not hot enough. Go do it again. Then there are the days, the horrible days, the days he sits staring out the window, his face wet.

Winnie, sometimes I think that I need you. Then sometimes I think that it is best if you don't come.

The loggers, he says. He cannot forget or forgive. He is consumed by it, the casual strike of saw against wood.

Of course they will not stop with the trees in Enchantment Bay, he says. They will move farther down the coast in a unstoppable advance. They will cut them all, cut them skinless and bleeding, gather them in huge rafts and send them south. We will see them as they pass the entrance to our bay, bundles of logs floating by. A forest in the water. Sometimes I think that you must stay far away from here.

I tell him if he wants to die, he must do it himself. But I know he will not. Another thing he has lost is his courage. He says that I need to be the one. This is the only thing he has ever asked of me, he says. If I truly love him, I will do it.

On those days, those rainy, dark days, I think of how I could kill him. A kitchen knife, slid between his ribs like butter. Rat poison, mixed with his food. A shrimp pot, cast deep in the ocean, a simple cut of the rope. There are a hundred ways to kill someone.

But I don't do any of them. Instead I bring him gifts from the forest that remains. A clump of orange fungus, a heart-shaped burl, mountain goat hair. I hope the forest will heal him. I hope that the things I bring to him will return the man I love to me. Each day I go farther and farther, past where I have ever been before, trying to find the cure.

He grows angry. "Why won't you do this one thing for me?" he asks. He ticks off ways: A pillow over the face. A hand pressing down in the bath. Not eating is too slow, he says. It has to be fast, he wants it over. Don't pay attention if I struggle, he warns me. Just keep doing it.

You need to choose, he says. You get to pick which way you want it.

Will you do it today? He asks. Is today the day?

No, I say. Not today.

Tomorrow?

Yes. Tomorrow.

Tomorrow it will start again.

I cannot talk to Sam; his face is turned away to see his idol brought to this. Sam does not want to know. He works instead, patching up things, long hours so he does not have to face this. Sam wishes for the old days even more than I do. He is lost too, a boy in a man's clothes.

I cannot share this with anyone but you.

The whales are back in the bay. I have waited for them for so long. It seems years since I last saw them. Their rounded backs are like big gray stones that I could step on, a pathway over the ocean. I can hear them breathe, a long sigh. I can see them breathe, a cold smoke.

Nothing changes here, not ever. The bears come and go with the salmon runs. The spring snow falls sweet and slow, melting in the warm breath of the forest. Nobody comes to the bay; it is only us with our old wounds.

I am like a seashell, curled up in a spiral. I am bloodless, drained, a pretty thing on a shelf. I listen and I try to understand. Soon I will know what the whales are trying to tell me.

I thought that I would never send this to you. But I want you to know what has happened to us. There is so much more I want to tell you, but it is too late now. The barge is coming. Ernie doesn't like to wait. The tide, he says. The tide is my mistress, he says, and laughs.

I long for you, Winnie, the days skin to skin, the days when you loved me. Come back. Do not come back.

I do not know which to choose.

There was no signature, and the words crowded the page as if she were eager to be done with them. Reading the letter, I saw what I had not before. The boundaries of mother and daughter had never been clearly defined. Instead my mother had wandered all over the map, taking me with her.

I had loved my father at times, despite the flashes of anger in the night, like lightning, unexpected and terrible, but gone the next day, nearly forgotten. Wasn't this the way life was? An avalanche could sweep down from the cliffs, sweeping a hillside clean of trees, but we grew used to the shorn mountain in a matter of days. The bears tussled and fought in the salmon streams, but the next day they pawed fish from the same water, shoulder to shoulder.

Reading the letter by flashlight, I felt a tug to my heart. Tomorrow would be the day that I would go back to Never Summer Bay. I would save them both. But then in the morning the eagles began their shrieks as the first brush of light touched the windows. Isaiah hummed in the kitchen, fixing cowboy coffee over the propane burner. On shore Birdman would be in the greenhouse because he said that being among young growing things made him hopeful. A cap of rain and fog lay tight over the bay. "What's the plan for today?" Isaiah would ask, smiling, and I would think: One more day. I deserve one more day of this. One more day with two old men who allow me to believe that all the anger in the world could be swallowed and never spit back out. One more day where I could decide who I was going to be—not Winnie, the girl from Never Summer Bay, but someone else, someone who never had to hide, ever again. And all of the one more days added up like flakes of snow added up to the immense weight of a glacier until it was nearly two years before I left Floathouse Bay.

Seven

I had been in Floathouse Bay for two winters, going on two springs, when the first boat came. Because nobody ever came in the bay, we had no time to react. In a minute it was upon us, a silver Lund moving like a bullet, sending a wash of foamy water over the dock. I did not expect to see the man who got out.

Isaiah and Birdman flanked me as Sam tied up the boat and got out. He nodded at them but fixed his eyes on me. "Buddy," he said, then corrected it. "Winnie. Long time."

Thoughts scattered like crabs on a beach. The same eyes, dark blue where sky met the sea. Same shaggy blond hair nearly covering those eyes. Same long fingers holding the rope. The same tingle that started in my toes and worked its way up.

"It has been," I managed. Had Sam come to bring me home? Had my father finally convinced my mother to do the impossible? No, I told myself. She would never do it.

For a second before he started to speak, I allowed myself to believe that he had come for me across five miles of rough water. He had come to rescue me, the same as in the old stories. On a few nights in Floathouse Bay I had spun an elaborate tale of how this would happen. But as soon as he spoke I felt the cold dash of disappointment. He had not come to rescue me. There was more trouble in Never Summer Bay.

Here in Floathouse Bay I had allowed myself to believe that nothing ever changed. The day slipped into night until months had passed without notice. Now I realized that outside of our sheltered place, life marched on at dizzying speed.

"Winnie. Roy sent me. I need you to come to Never Summer with me."

Immediately I thought of the sly low tide and its mate, the flood, and suspected a trick. I thought of the woman on the tide flats, seduced out farther and farther on the wide sweet expanse of beach, the water pulled back like a curtain to reveal what had been there all along.

"Listen," he said as I stood waiting, my mind skipping through possibilities. "Your mother, she's missing. Althea didn't come back last night or the night before that. I suppose you know things have gotten bad in Never Summer. No more clients, selling everything off that we can, hoping for a turnaround. News gets out, nobody will hunt with him anymore. I was sticking around until next winter to help them out. But she's gone somewhere, and I need your help."

I listen and I try to understand. Soon I will know what the whales are trying to tell me.

Wouldn't I know if my mother had been swallowed up by the country? I would feel it, the snap of the rope. But so much time had gone by. Two years, a lifetime. Had our bond frayed beyond repair? There was this too: This place could seduce you into taking chances, the way it bent out of sight just enough that you wanted to see what was past the next bend, up the next mountain. There were so many ways to die out here. A slip on slimy deer cabbage, arms windmilling as you tumbled down a mountain. A boulder falling as you reached for it, smashing your ankle. Bears waking up from a long sleep. Rivers running chalky with glacier melt. Even the rain, slowly filtering in through your best gear, your fingers growing stiff as you try to start a fire. You never, ever went very far on land alone, not if you wanted to come back, no matter how much you wanted to go on. No matter how much you wanted to put the past behind you and run.

"Are you sure she's not just waiting out the weather, or high and dry on a beach?" I asked. Both things had happened to us many times.

"I don't think so. Not this time."

Isaiah said, "I don't like the sound of this. Search and Rescue has an office in town. Call them. Radiophone still works up in the lodge, right?"

"No can do," Sam said. "They won't come. You've heard what they say up and down the coast. Nobody's going to come here. Not even Search and Rescue. They've looked the other way for years. He's a loose cannon, they say. He burned all his bridges long ago."

"They would come," Isaiah argued. But I knew Sam was right. After the search was called off for Uncle Dean, my father had taken the barge around the island to town and stormed into Search and Rescue's office. Only a set of burly troopers had been able to steer him out before blows were exchanged. My father, returning, had told the story as if he were the hero.

"Nobody would help us," I said. "We never helped anyone else." Never veered over to check on fishing boats in trouble, never offered to sell anyone extra fuel like I had heard the other settlements did. In the other small outposts scattered up and down the coast, travelers knew who would come to their aid. From the fish weir, a dip net full of salmon for the hungry. At the field camp, a bunk inside a wall tent for the shipwrecked. But everyone knew to avoid Never Summer Bay or else end up with extra lead in their boats. Nobody would help him now, even the most kindhearted.

In Never Summer Bay, we had always been on our own too. The time one of the skiffs had broken loose of the dock and floated out of the bay on an ebb tide, Sam and my father had to go hunt for it, finding it washed up on one of the Harbor Islands. Nobody, finding it, would have brought it back. Nobody would come help cut beach logs or reshingle the roof. Got what he deserved, the bastard, they would have said, and meant it.

We stood in an unsteady cluster. Glancing up at Isaiah and Birdman, I knew they would not choose for me, although I could feel their words, unspoken, like clouds of unshed rain: *Don't ever go back.*

I remembered the words she had said to me.

"I would dive into the water, holding on to your back. We would swim through the ocean, blowing bubbles. You wouldn't be afraid, because I would never leave you."

Don't ever go back.
You must stay away from here.

There was the rush of water under the dock, making the decision for me. Flood tide. Insistent. Stronger than a person could row, stronger even than the push of an outboard. Pretty soon it would drain out from the bay, trapping the four of us for hours as we waited it out.

I saw my mother, her hair the color of moonlight. I saw her in a kayak next to mine near the Trader Islands, our paddles dipping into transparent liquid. I saw her, chin cupped in hand, watching the ocean worry the shore. I saw her as we wandered the beach fringe. Behind us the bears had moved like shadows in the forest. We were part of the bay, she had told me, as much a part of it as the gulls and the otters and the sea stars. You could not see the place where any of it ended and we began. "When I die, don't put me in a box," she had told me once. "Scatter me like pieces of the sun in the ocean. Promise me, Winnie. Promise me."

There was no choice. There never had been.

"I have to go," I said. "I promised her I would. All of my life I promised her."

Isaiah only nodded. "I know," he said. "Old promises are the hardest to break."

I thought that Birdman had disappeared into the greenhouse, the place he went to hide, but he was standing next to me with an ancient army pack strapped to his back. "Hold up. I'm going with you."

Isaiah shook his head once. I could tell they were using their secret language, the one where they did not need words. *This isn't your fight. Stay here.*

Birdman knew what Isaiah was trying to say. But he looked away as if embarrassed to reveal his soft interior. "She's like my daughter now, Isaiah," he said. "I look at her and I see Angela. Couldn't live with myself if I let her go off without one of us to watch over her."

Something unfamiliar squeezed my heart tight.

"Birdman, you need to stay here. You belong here," I said. He was such a small man, so close to bone. How could I bring him to a place like Never Summer Bay?

He crossed his arms across his chest. "You need a tracker, someone to find sign. How many hours have you spent in the high country? It's a different world than down here on the beach."

It was true. "He never let us go past the muskeg," I said. "It wasn't safe, he told us. Stay down by the sea, he said."

"Do you know how to find your way through a cedar flat, either of you?" Birdman's gesture took in both Sam and me. "Do you know how to walk across a snowfield without it falling away under your feet? What tracks will you miss, the two of you?"

"Birdman," Isaiah said, a warning. His fingers grasped Birdman's coat sleeve as if he was trying to hold him back.

"Nobody else will die in the woods because I wasn't there to save them," Birdman replied, and from the way Isaiah stepped back, letting his hand fall, I knew there was a decades-old story they both remembered. I knew that whatever story was unfurling now had begun long before I was born.

"He goes," Sam said. He took hold of the bow line. "We'd best go now before the flood tide."

Isaiah clapped me on the shoulder, not meeting my eyes. "I can't go there and get caught up in that trouble again, understand? It's like the sticky mud in the estuary. Grabs hold of a guy and it's hell to get free. But come back," he said. "When this is over, come back."

I knew nobody ever came back to Floathouse Bay. Mostly, Isaiah had said, people who had sheltered here wanted to reinvent themselves after leaving. They wanted to forget the circumstances that had made them need such a place. They wanted to sail on, no baggage, toward the rest of their lives.

Isaiah and Birdman exchanged another glance. One man asked a question with his eyes, the other nodded. A lifetime passed between them.

"Remember this, Winnie," Isaiah said. "You may be no bigger than a pint jar of whiskey, but you're stronger than you know. You have steel inside of you. It will be there when you reach down for it. Don't you ever forget that."

I did not see what he saw. Instead I felt anything but strong as I stepped into the swaying skiff, steadied by Sam's arm. I was as weak as one of the early flowers that were fooled by the spring, my legs barely strong enough to hold me.

Isaiah stood with arms folded as we cast off our line. "Good luck," he hollered over the sound of the engine. We were going to need every ounce of good luck there was.

We motored slowly out of the bay, our wake hitting the dock with a gentle slap. As we passed them the cormorants rose from their perch and filled the sky with black feathers. Their wings had finally dried enough for them to fly.

As the three of us steamed north, crammed uncomfortably in a boat that banged hard on each wave, I could see everything that I once knew by heart. There was the low cluster of islands we had called the Maze, a confusing puzzle of wandering channels and dead ends. There was the beach where we used to gather driftwood logs, towing them behind the boat for firewood. There was the good halibut hole and the shelves where we had found the best abalones.

This is my homeland.

I understood what Isaiah had meant in the muskeg.

Five miles had seemed so long when I was younger, an improbable expanse of water to cross. Now five miles took only minutes for us to plot a course through. I sat in the bow scanning the horizon for rogue logs that could pin us in seconds, spinning the boat in a death spiral. The wind forced my eyes to tear. We passed the rocks where the sea lions lived and the kelp-strewn place where whales hunted and jumped right out of the water, arcing in one smooth motion before sliding beneath the surface of the sea. We passed all the spots where we could have turned back.

The boat could have taken on water from a rogue wave, making us stop to bail. The engine could have sputtered from lack of fuel. We could have come up hard on a rock. All of those things had happened before. This time nothing stopped us. The tide and the wind turned in our favor, as if conspiring to shorten the journey.

Before I was ready we made the sharp turn into Never Summer Bay, the craggy red cliffs guarding the entrance slipping past us too quickly. Stop, I wanted to say, go slower. Let me breathe.

As if he heard me, Sam idled the motor past the red cliffs. Uncharted rocks lay beneath the surface and more than one assistant guide had ground up a prop on them. "Wait," I said. I had forgotten to ask. *You'll have a brother in the spring.*

"Were there other children, after I left?" But Sam just shook his head, puzzled. "There were no babies," he said. "What made you think that there were?"

"No reason." Another story she had made up to plaster over the truth, that it would always just be the three of us in the bay forever? Or had it been true for only a short time, and then not? There was no way to know.

We ground to a stop on the cobble beach. I was home.

I scrambled out of the boat to pull the line to shore. Sam had chosen the beach for landing; the dock looked barely stable, good enough for walking but not strong enough to hold a boat turning in the tide. I stepped out too soon and cold water seeped over the top of my boots. That was the excuse I gave for freezing in place while I stood on one leg, draining out cold sea from each one.

"What's happened here?" Birdman said. I saw it too. Things were worse in the bay than any of us had ever imagined.

Here was the place where I had lived for seventeen years. Coming back here should have felt like the inside of a well-worn glove. Instead nothing looked the same.

Eight

The forest had forgiven us. In the time since I had been gone, it had begun to heal over the places that we had hacked and burned and carved out so we could live here. Alder had bullied in, creating a fortress along the shore, a wall of intertwined limbs hiding what remained of the lodge. Storm tides had broken up the dock, tossing boards up into the beach fringe. Only a skeleton of it remained, barely safe to walk on.

Moss and bears had worked together to bring down the boathouse. Small scavenging creatures had stolen the beach glass collection that my mother kept on the deck railing. Little by little everything that was ours was vanishing.

Nothing was permanent, even the sea. Years ago the ocean covered this stretch of beach and the forest above it. Exploring, we had found the old shorelines; stark, wave-scoured cliffs now crumbling slowly under the weight of trees; small insistent streams carving down through the exposed rock. Even now, thirteen thousand years after the last ice sheets retreated, the earth was still rising about an inch per year, expanding upward like a pair of lungs, the land taking in a long, deep breath. What I saw here now would not be the same for long. Standing on an uncertain shore I was reminded of the elusiveness of everything.

How could it have changed so much, so fast? But I knew that was the way things worked here. It took constant vigilance to carve out a space on this coast. You had to endlessly work to fit yourself in here between the devil's club and the landslides and the tide. The second you turned your back it bested you. It always would.

Sam cut the engine and lifted the dripping outboard, and we stood for a moment in the silence. It took a few minutes to hear the sounds of the bay again; the delicate lick of waves on the shore, the crackling of barnacles exposed to light.

I had forgotten so much. I had forgotten the red cliffs, the way they dropped abruptly into the sea below.

That was not the only thing I had forgotten. I had forgotten the way the air felt, somehow different in this bay than in all of the others, thick with unshed water, almost liquid enough to drink. I had forgotten how my feet could sink deep below the high tide line. I had forgotten the bodies of moon jellyfish and the splayed, fat legs of purple sea stars as they were abandoned by the falling water.

I had not known there was so much to forget.

Without thinking, I grasped Sam's hand for courage. Birdman did not seem to need any. Instead he stepped away from us and trudged the shore, looking up at the cliffs and studying them carefully. He spoke to himself as he walked, making a map in his head.

Sam glanced down at the place where our hands met.

"All it did was rain after you left, Winnie," he said. "Seems like all of the sunshine was drawn out of this bay. We missed you here."

"Even you?"

"I never knew how much until you were gone."

In days past I would have pulled these words in close to my chest, tumbled them through my hands like beach glass, and searched them for hidden meaning. There was no time for that now.

"What will be it like in there?"

Sam looked uncomfortable. He dropped my hand. "He'll have heard us come in. You know how he doesn't like to wait."

I did know. Patience had never been my father's strong suit. He was often whipped into a frenzy he had to swallow down hard, irritated by the way the clients inched down the steep ramp in tiny mincing steps, or how they took forever fussing with their rifles when it was time to shoot. When we were slow, too, he turned on us with words that cut like a bitter wind.

"He may tell you the story of what happened in Enchantment Bay. If he does, come find me. Promise me."

I had heard so many promises in this bay. Promises were hollow words, hollow as the bones of birds, easily broken. Isaiah and Birdman had promised a score of women they would stay and had left each one. My father had promised a string of days without anger. Promises had brought me back to where I stood, irresolute on a familiar beach.

"You'll find him different. He's not the same man you knew."

My fingers remembered Sam's touch. It had been a long time since I had touched anyone that way. Isaiah and Birdman skirted the edges of decorum, treating me like a daughter, sometimes merely resting a gnarled hand on my head. I was used to the unforgiving—the harsh slap of a rope in salt-cut hands or the splintered wood of the floathouse walls. I was acquainted with that toughness now and had thought I could live without the other. Now I knew I was wrong.

"How is he different?" *A gray-faced ghost.* I wasn't sure if I was capable of taking a step. The man I had known was mercurial but recognizable. I had learned to forecast how to move around him by little signs he gave us. We had weathered each mood as though it were a gale or a day of unexpected sun. I wasn't sure how to navigate someone new.

Sam spun me around and gave me a little push. "Winnie. Go. I'm right behind you. I'll be here if you need me."

Nobody came down the path like they would have in the old days, my father hurrying down with either a cart or a shotgun, depending on which it was, friend or enemy, and a dark dog in the series of Labradors we had kept tight at his heels. But now there was only silence as I struggled through the alders. The path was overgrown, only an indentation in the solid mass of brush that separated the beach fringe from the forest. The boardwalk was skimmed over with moss and was missing a few planks. The bushes we had always kept pruned slapped my thin jacket and my face as if warning me to turn back.

"It all got away from us," Sam said behind me. "Neither of us realized how much Roy did until he couldn't do it anymore." It was true that my father had rarely been still. Even when the clients were gone he had worked, a wrench stuffed in his back pocket, hands curled around an ax. "Daylight's burning," he had called to us en route to another errand, rousing my mother and me from our lazy afternoons.

A man sat on the porch in a wheelchair. He wore a wool hat pulled down over his head and his eyes were closed, as if he were dozing. It was an old man, nobody I knew, I tried to tell myself, but the lie didn't work. This was my father.

As I walked closer it was clear that he had been in a terrible accident. A patchwork of scars ran the length of the right side of his face, puckering the skin. When his eyes blinked open I saw that one was made of blue glass. The other was a dark brown, nearly black. The effect was both repelling and fascinating.

"Hope to shout," my father said a little above a whisper. This was a phrase I had heard all through my childhood. I had never known what it meant exactly, but it was said when something surprising happened—a barn-door halibut on the end of the line, orcas following the boat. It meant that good things were happening, and as long as the good things continued, I could let down my guard a little. The good things would string along an invisible line like laundry, adding up to how long? A week? A month?

"Well, look who decided to show her face," he said.

I moved a little closer, trying to reconcile this old man with the one I had known. His voice was the same but that was all. The man I had known could never have been like this. Heat had radiated off his body as he strode from room to room, his mind brimming with ideas. He had stood at the bottom of the steps, coat in hand, boots on. It was three in the morning, just turning light in summer, the birds just beginning to sing. "Get your asses up. It's a fine day in paradise!" he yelled, rousing the clients from their beds.

Back then, he was forever afraid of missing out. The clients trailed in his wake, blistered and exhausted, but carried along in a river of enthusiasm.

This wasn't the same man, sitting here deflated like a balloon, a blanket resting on his knees.

"You look just like her. I'd forgotten just how much."

I had forgotten too, surer in my own body in Floathouse Bay than I had ever been here. I had not been a reflection of my mother there but someone whole.

"I wanted to come earlier," I said, which had sometimes been true. "It never was the right time." And there had always been a reason not to go, though I did not say so. Crabs to harvest from the sea, deer to stalk, the icy touch of winter. As I said this I could hear how flimsy the words were. Surely my father would see right through them, but he only waved a hand in dismissal.

"Ancient history, Winchester. Old news. You couldn't have done anything if you had been here. Everyone's heard all about it, up and down the coast. They've moved on to different stories now. Sam here can fill you in on what you don't know. Can't you, Sam?"

Sam looked at the warped boards and said nothing.

"Could have used an extra hand, though," my father went on. "First year you left, we had a windstorm that threw trees like matchsticks. One big one collapsed the boathouse, and we gave up on it then. Left it open to the weather. Last spring, we had extreme high tides, the kind that sometimes come during the full moon. Those didn't do the dock any favors. Place has gone to hell in a handbasket."

He rolled toward the open door, motioning me to follow. His arms propelled the chair in a slow and measured way as if there was an old wound deep in his bones that he was trying to avoid disturbing.

I swallowed back my questions. My father had never given up information easily. "You're on a need-to-know basis," he had always told the clients. "It's my way or the highway out here. I come to New York, God forbid, you can boss me around there. Here I'm in charge." Always they fell into line, meekly rolling up their sleeping bags when he gave the order. My mother and I had fallen into line, too.

My father had built the house from the land and sea, using as much as he could from the bay and forest itself, bringing everything else in by barge. That way the wood would weather with the elements as if it were a part of the forest, he had instructed me when I asked how he had done it. Though he had nearly broken his back clearing a space, he told me that some things you had to work with instead of against, and building a house here was one of those things. Avalanche, windstorm, tsunami—you had to think about the possibility of each of these and adjust what you wanted to what could be.

Being in the lodge was like living inside a large tree. I had always loved the building, with its spiral staircase leading to our rooms, the open great room with panes of windows from earth to sky, and the bumbling stairs that led to the clients' small quarters. He had no experience and only an instruction book on house building and he had gotten some of it wrong, but somehow the uneven floors and doors that opened by themselves worked together to create a unique house.

Because of the way it was built, my mother and I had found many hiding places. They were small, tucked-away rooms that nobody used but that provided shelter while my father wore himself out raging over trouble that had occurred that day. Often we sat with knees tucked up to our chins, telling stories while heavy footsteps and spilt ice cubes rattled the floor overhead. *What if a prince on a white horse rode up asking if any beautiful young girls lived here? What if apples fell from the sky instead of rain? What would you do then?*

Everything looked the same, the copper-colored beams that my father had cut and planed himself, the brown bear hide draped over the back of the homemade cedar sofa, the deep windows where my mother used to sit and look out at the rain. But something was different too, a taste to the air, a bitter smell of mold and regret.

Despite this, I suddenly felt like time had never passed. I was ten years old again, a little girl hiding behind her bangs. At any moment I expected Uncle Dean to taxi up to the dock, clients steaming up the windows of his plane, their doughy faces pressed up to the Plexiglas. I expected to see bear skins hanging off the rail of the boat, ready for sealing, hear loud laughter of the men and feel the damp closeness of the nightfall around us. I expected to feel the same seesaw of emotions, the fear of what would come next. Standing here now I felt that the past was coming up behind me like an old cloak. It would shrug itself on over my shoulders and I would never be able to get free.

There was an awkward pause. I could hear the kitchen clock ticking in the silence.

"Treated you all right down coast?" he asked. "I knew they would. We fell out years ago, but their hearts are good down there."

"I love them," I said, feeling strangely disloyal. It was a different kind of love than I had ever known, a subtle drip of water from a hidden seep instead of a torrent. The words hung in the air and for a moment nobody spoke.

"No pedestals on the coast," my father said finally. I could see a hint of what I thought was old anger in his face, or maybe hurt. "Those boys have just as much history as the rest of us. All of us came here looking for something or running from something. Sometimes it's both."

I knew he was right; ghosts chased Isaiah and Birdman. They had lived five decades and their pasts sometimes haunted them, sneaking up unaware as we drank coffee. At those times they cleared their throats and shuffled out to the dock, their backs rounded against whatever burdens they carried.

"Well," he said, "you're back now. Just in time. I need your help."

"So where is she?" I asked. I looked at my father, upright in his chair, studying me as closely as I was looking at him. *Did you do something to her? Something bad?* I wasn't brave enough to say it aloud, not here, not yet. I didn't want to believe it either, and saying it would make it a possibility. And there was this: how could he have hurt my mother? Look at him, his legs like sticks under the blanket.

She had started hiking a few weeks ago, he told me. At first, he said, she only disappeared for an hour, then two, then a whole day. "At first she only went to the bluff," he told me. "The next day she started going farther, up to the muskeg and just where the cedar flats begin. Soon she was gone for most of the day. But she always came back."

She brought him stories like gifts. The way the lichens hung like blonde women's hair off the trees, silver drops of rain caught in a spider's web. Early spring bear tracks in the snow, crossing over the pass. She brought things back too, placing them in his cupped hands. A shredded balloon, found tangled in devil's club, blown in from who knew where. The first shoot of swamp cabbage. An antler. "She knew how much I missed being out there," he said. "She told me she was bringing the forest back to me."

I could see her doing this, her arms full of gifts, hoping each one would make him better.

"I told him that maybe she crossed the island to town," Sam said. "I mean, Roy, you have to consider the possibility that maybe she left and doesn't want to come back."

"Nobody's ever crossed the island and made it alive," my father answered. "There are five-thousand-foot peaks to get over. You'd have to cross the Despair River. Swim, probably, this time of year, with all the snowmelt. The alder is such a thick mat that you'd never even touch the ground. Devil's club higher than your head. Waterfalls taller than God. It's impossible country up there. Dean and I flew it a million times, enough to know what it's like. No, I think she is in trouble. The longer we spend talking about it, the less time we have to find her."

In the silence that followed I heard only the rain. It dripped off the rotting wood shingles and rolled down the windows, splashing into the moss on the stairs. It seemed insistent, worming its way through the weak places of the house.

"Where are the other boats?" I asked.

Sam said, "Sold. Broken. Gone. She didn't leave by sea."

If my mother had left by land, she must have meant to come back. She hadn't been leaving for good. Like my father had said, nobody could walk across the island. It had been tried before, a couple times. Both times, the men—and they had all been men, adventurers from somewhere else—had vanished, an extensive air search locating nothing but the remains of a tent wrapped around a tree. Ernie brought us those grim tales, and we had all secretly thought that those men had gotten what they deserved. Who were they to challenge a wilderness that was older than time? My mother would not walk across the island, I thought. She would remember the stories. Where had she gone?

Not the muskeg. She had been there a hundred times. Although you could fall in the muskeg, pinned under the weight of your pack in a bottomless pool, drowning in only a few feet of water, she knew the muskeg and where to walk in it. Instead, she was gathering up her courage to go farther and farther. Perhaps she wanted to bring my father more elaborate gifts each time: stones that used to live at the bottom of a river, bark from a thousand-year-old tree. Something that would work.

What was past the muskeg? I knew that there was a wall of cedar, too thick for us ever to penetrate. Beyond that, there was only a blank space on the map I carried in my head. I thought there might have been a river, the source of one of the many streams that bubbled out into the bay. Where did the river come from?

A memory emerged. I knew where my mother had gone.

I went to the cabinet that had always held the topographic maps. They were still there, tightly rolled in cracking elastic bands, neatly labeled in my mother's cramped handwriting. I pulled out the right one and unfolded it on the table. Age and humidity curled the edges, and I anchored those using copies of the *Coast Pilot*.

"It's called the Lake of the Fallen Moon," I told Sam. "See it here, just above the red cliffs and below the divide? This waterfall must come from the lake. Uncle Dean used to talk about this lake. What if she went there?"

At ten years old I had liked to think of Uncle Dean at Lake of the Fallen Moon. Maybe he had changed his mind partway around the island, made a U-turn, and headed there, deciding to transform his life, to start over.

"What do you think Uncle Dean's doing now?" I would ask, starting the story.

My mother would think for a moment. Her eyes were sad. "Picking blueberries. He'll make a pie. And ice cream, from snow."

"He's probably built a cabin by now," I guessed. "Maybe he's made a canoe."

Deep down I knew that Uncle Dean was really under two hundred feet of water, his plane tumbling along the bottom of the ocean in the restless current, but it was easier to imagine him at Lake of the Fallen Moon instead.

Sam had been leaning over the map. Now he stood up, rubbing his eyes. He had never taken up much space, but now I noticed that his Carhartts hung looser on his hips than they ever had. He looked as though he had not slept in days. "Well, I don't know," he said. "It isn't far past the red cliffs. One night at the most, maybe two days' walk. It doesn't seem like much to go on, just a hunch. I mean, you were a little girl then. What do you think, Roy?"

Sam had never been a forceful person, not like the series of headstrong assistant guides that had preceded him. He could be talked into a lot of things: leaving shore in the remnants of a gale, climbing higher into rain-soaked creeks. It was a quality that my father liked. "Finally got a keeper," he told us. Now I wondered if Sam had also been chosen because he would never speak out; the secrets of our bay would be held close to his chest like a hand of cards.

My father stabbed a finger at the contours on the map. "Look at how steep it is. She couldn't have made it up there. I've been up on those cliffs. The rock crumbles off in your hands. I saw Jesus a time or two on those cliffs."

I leaned in and tried to make sense of the map. I only knew how to read charts, the language of the sea. Sometimes the charts showed the blue outline of interior lakes or significant features like the red cliffs, but for the most part the land itself wasn't what we studied. We had kept a full set of topographic maps just in case a wounded bear had left the beach fringe and climbed high, but we had hardly ever used them. Back then, the only geography that was important to know was that of water.

Thin brown lines bracketed the tiny bowl where the lake sat. Close together, so close that there was barely any white space. Steep. Too steep, my father proclaimed. Only birds could get there, he said.

He had always forbidden us from climbing the red cliffs. Dangerous rocks, he said, the same kind that beat near the earth's core. Compasses spun wildly there and strange plants found nowhere else clustered in tiny crevices. It was not a place for us to go. Better to stay by the sea, where he could make sure we were safe.

My mother had agreed quickly. She was cautious of the land. She had ticked off all the ways that water had tried to kill her, but she still preferred the sea. Riptides, following sea, your foot caught in a rope, she had said. I'll take those over what the land might serve up.

"Looks like a hell of a climb," Sam said. Worry scribbled across his face. He had always hung on my father's heels like the Labs. He had never taken a trip alone. I had never been farther than the muskeg.

Birdman lingered behind us, studying the bay. Now he stepped inside the lodge. I watched a storm play out on my father's face and braced myself, but then he looked resigned. "You brought him. Best tracker in Alaska. I would have done the same."

"Long time, Roy," Birdman said. "I see you've gotten yourself into a spot of trouble."

To my surprise my father laughed, throwing his head back. For a minute he was the man I remembered, teeth a flash of white in his dark face, eyes snapping. "Always had a way with words," he said. "Come to save the day, have you?"

"Lake of the Fallen Moon," Sam cut in. "But there's the red cliffs. We don't know about the red cliffs."

"There's a way around those cliffs," Birdman said calmly. "I studied them for a bit, the way they come down through the cedars up high. We'll still have some climbing to do, but we can sneak up on them through the muskeg and the cedar. I think we can make it to that lake, if that's where you're wanting to go."

"Are you sure?"

He nodded, not even glancing at the map.

"Everything I know, I learned from Birdman," my father said, surprising me again. I had never thought of my father as a student. It always seemed he was born knowing the coast, but now I realized he must have had a teacher. Had he walked through the same valleys with Birdman that I had, learning the stories in the sand? Had they stood back to back, trusting each other with their lives? How had he answered the one question that Birdman always asked?

"You can go up the cliffs that way, if he says you can," my father said. "I've never tried it that way. Always did it the hard way, from the water, and a guy has got to have more guts than any of you have. But Birdman can read the country like nobody else I've ever known. The lake, though, I'd advise against it. Nothing good can come out of going there."

Birdman's gaze was steady. "What is it about the lake you are afraid of, Roy?"

My father's eyes dropped first. I had never seen that before, not ever, even with the sturdiest, most demanding client.

"I'm only allowing it because I want you to find her," he said. "Go on to the lake then. Find whatever you're going to find there. I still think it's a dangerous endeavor."

With his grudging approval, hope galvanized me. My mother was perhaps only a day's walk away. A pile of gear grew around us as Sam carried armfuls from the closet. What would we need to climb so high? Each piece of gear carried a memory with it. The tiny stove had brewed up coffee during our driftwood gathering expeditions. I had slid inside one of these sleeping bags when my mother and I camped on the Trader Islands to dive for abalone. We had walked toward each other and away in a kind of dance, folding up a tarp like the ones I sorted through now.

"It will be what it has to be," my father said. "You leave as soon as you are ready." He rose to his feet, holding the back of the chair behind him, wavering slightly. I remembered the way he used to be, strong muscles working under the rough fabric of his shirt as he lifted the anchor, a ground-eating stride that could leave anyone in his wake. Now he shuffled, uncertain. He was suddenly old, bent like a comma. He didn't stand for long before he dropped back into the chair.

I knew he was recalling days gone by and after a minute he said, "Remember, Winnie, the old days? When we would gather around the charts and talk about the weather and which bays to anchor in? Remember all the wives, and how they couldn't decide whether to go along or stay here in the lodge? Carrying all of their stuff, duffels and duffels of it, down to the boat while they watched us? Remember how it was?"

"How could I forget?" Through it all we had, all of us—the clients, my mother, myself—spun around my father like planets to a sun.

My father went on as if I hadn't spoken. "It took hours but we would fire up the boat and the clients would be huddled up there in the pilothouse with their binocs, sharp smell of nervous sweat so bad I made them go out on the deck. When we got back after the hunt, they would jump off the boat and they were different men then. Conquerors. Kissing the wives like returning heroes. It was something to see. And I made that happen for them."

His knobby hands were folded in his lap as the rest of us picked through gear. "You know, this was always a hardscrabble operation. Close to the edge. Everything was fixed with duct tape and baling wire. Things barely ran. We were always out there in the rain and saltwater fixing something. But the clients, they never saw that. The trips changed them forever," he said. "Remember, Winnie?"

I remembered. I watched him covertly as I divided up the gear into three old frame backpacks and gave Birdman and Sam their share. Something flickered across his face that I could not understand. I might have called it regret, if my father had been that kind of man.

I had imagined that if I ever went home that things would have gone very differently. There would have been old hurts to navigate, storms to weather. Doors might have slammed, words tossed like anchors through hallways. This was almost worse. Regret hung around the lodge, thick as fog.

I turned my back on him and went in search of food we could carry. Slipping through the door into the walk-in pantry, more like a room than a closet, I stifled a gasp. The pantry had been the heart of the house. It had been stuffed full with jars of every color like floating jewels. There had been the translucent pink of canned salmon and flaky white halibut. There were the deep purple of beets and orange globes of peaches. We had made elaborate meals for the clients, biscuits with rosemary and sage, whole salmon marinated in lemon, pitchers of sweet tea. We ordered boxes and boxes of groceries each week, puffing up the ramp with the carts. We gathered the best salmonberries and the ripest blueberries for pies and had stewed young venison for hours in a big cast-iron pot. Nobody ever went hungry at Never Summer Lodge. Now there were only a few suspect apples and boxes of instant oatmeal and spaghetti.

Sam followed me, pulling the pantry door shut behind him. He saw me looking at the empty shelves. "Ernie still came in now and then," he said. "He dropped off what food we could afford. I chipped in what I could. We weren't starving, if that's what you're thinking."

"Why didn't they leave? They could have gone someplace else, started over where nobody knew him."

"Leave how?"

"There was the barge. Ernie would have taken them out."

"You really think he would leave here?"

Sam was right. My father wouldn't ever leave, I knew, no matter how bad things got. I couldn't picture him anywhere else, especially not in a place where pavement replaced the ocean and buildings blocked out the sky. He would never survive.

Kitchen light spilled through the door slats, painting Sam's face in stripes of darkness and gold.

I leaned toward him like a plant seeking sun. Something drew me closer, something I could not name but which felt familiar as air. It was the same feeling as the tickle of ferns on bare skin and the shiver of cold water down my throat. I knew next to nothing about him, but I knew I was different than the women in the pictures he had sent us from Panama over the winter. They had glossy hair caught in buns, smooth bodies bursting out of scraps of fabric. My hair was snarled and wild down my back, and I wore someone else's clothes. Even the women's eyes looked wiser than mine would ever be.

I imagined how he talked about me. *There was this kid. I don't know, fifteen? Seventeen tops. Had a crush on me. Followed me around all the time. Couldn't shake her.*

One of the women would run a fingernail down his bare back. "Sweet," she would say. "What was her name?"

And he would tell her, and she would giggle. "Named after a rifle? What kind of people are they out there in Alaska?"

Still, I thought that he might lean closer, meet me halfway. There was that sense I had as a younger girl, a sense of understanding between us, something unexplainable but as real as the jar in my hands. I thought that he might close the distance between us without saying a single word.

Sam leaned back against the wall. The spell was broken. He was not going to kiss me. "Tell me everything," he said. "We are risking our lives out there, and I need to know everything that you know."

What stopped him? I glanced over my shoulder.

My father and Birdman sat in the room behind us, amber glasses full of liquid at their elbows. They spoke so low that I couldn't hear, maps spread out before them. Old wars seemed forgotten, only lost years between them now. I knew they watched our shadows through the slats of the pantry door.

My mother was missing. I should not be thinking about anything other than that. I should not be counting the distance that separated me from a man I had always thought I loved, even if he had never loved me back.

"I asked her once where her mother was," I said, remembering that day. We were paddling through the Trader Islands, just shy of the rip current she said would carry me away forever. Thirteen. I had begun to think about a world beyond the boundaries we had carefully laid out for ourselves.

"What did she say?"

"She said that it was a place where people cared more about what showed on the outside than what went on behind closed doors. She said, and it almost seemed like a warning, 'I was a great disappointment to my mother.' And she told me that I should not mention her again, because it bruised her heart."

I left out the last part, where my mother had laid her paddle across her boat and reached over to grasp my hand. "Winnie," she had said, "we will never be like my mother and me. We'll be together forever. Promise me." And because we were drifting too close to the current, because I had always believed that my mother needed protecting, I had promised.

"They talked about this bay like it was the only place in the world," I said. "Their stories were always about being here, never about the past."

Sam said, "I know about trying to forget where you came from." Before I could ask what that meant, he said quickly, "Do you remember her talking to anyone? Could she have told anyone where she was going?"

"You were here long after me. Was there someone?"

Sam ticked off people on his fingers. "Ernie?"

"Not Ernie. He never got in the middle of any of the stories. He just liked to tell the stories, but then he was on his way before any trouble stuck."

"You're right. Never stayed long enough for us to miss him." He considered. "The pilots were just loading butts into the aircraft as fast as they could before the weather came down. We never even learned their names."

"The radiophone? Did you still use the radiophone?"

"They stopped using the radiophone after the accident," Sam said, and I knew that she would never have tried to be saved that way. A lifeline for the coast dwellers, it crackled with private conversation, grocery orders, and gossip. Anyone could listen in to what you said, and the next day everyone would know your business. There had been too much danger in the radiophone.

We had kept the marine radio on, tuned to channel 16, and sometimes passing boats hailed us, wanting shelter or fuel. My father answered in a clipped tone, sending them away. "Five miles down the coast," he would tell them, clenching the microphone. "Try Floathouse Bay. We have nothing left to give here."

"What about where he came from?" Sam asked, but I knew there would be no help there either.

"When I wondered once why I didn't have grandparents, his face went dark. He said they were dried up and sour as month-old apples. They never came here, even when Uncle Dean disappeared. My father said they blamed him, as if he had made my uncle fly into the storm."

There was nobody, and Sam and I both knew it.

Sam reached out, tucked a strand of hair behind my ear. "What do you think, Winnie? Did she run?"

The place where his hand had touched must surely be burning bright red. I stared at my toes. There were no answers. In my heart I believed that my mother had gone to the Lake of the Fallen Moon. There was no real reason to believe it, but I pictured her there, blueberries staining her mouth the color of the ocean. Perhaps she had lost track of time. Perhaps she never meant to come back. We would never know unless we went there.

Sam said, "I really don't think she would go that far. I was just out there listening. Roy's hard to read, as usual. He seems to think that the lake is unreachable, but if there's a chance she got there, he wants us to go. Birdman talks about the cedars like they are impossible to pass through. I know he can do it, but what about us? What about her? She was as thin as a plate. Arms so little I could circle them with two fingers, I bet. Then you have the cliffs, and I've boated close enough to them to know that they'll crumble under you if you choose the wrong route. You have to be sure. Are you?"

I would be taking him and Birdman on a possibly dangerous route. None of us had scouted this country or sized it up. We had no idea what lay ahead. This was all based on a story my mother had told, a game we had played. I had learned that many of her stories were as ephemeral as the waterfalls that poured down the sides of the bay in summer, just a memory when the rain ceased.

I had never been less sure of anything. My mother and I filled the hours with so many words. The lake was just one place, one story in a thousand stories we created about the land around us. Stories, I realized, were how we had moved through the landscape. Stories had made this big, impossible country easier to understand.

"We have to try. How can we not try?"

Sam exhaled in a short burst. He slapped his hand against a shelf. "Well, you can't go by yourself up there. I don't like going against what Roy says. He hasn't steered me wrong yet, and there's something about that lake he doesn't care for. But I don't have any better ideas, and I owe it to him to find her. We'll go to the Lake of the Fallen Moon."

He scooped up the food and started to shoulder his way out of the pantry. Then he paused.

"Winnie, there is a lot I want to say to you. Things you should know. But not here, not now. Can you wait?"

Like the cormorants, I was good at waiting. Sometimes it seemed as though I had spent my whole life waiting. Sometimes I thought that waiting was less perilous than making the irrevocable decision to fly.

Birdman and my father tipped their glasses, heads flung back. The level of liquid in the bottle lowered by inches with each sloppy pour. They stoked the fire high and the woodstove glowed cherry red. They opened the windows to combat the heat, and the clean smell of leftover rain filled the room.

Whiskey loosened their tongues. Dots of color bloomed in Birdman's cheeks. He told us of events that had happened long before I was born. They were adventures that occurred before the trouble, a handful of men alone in a forgotten bay at the end of the world.

"Roy, remember the time when you flew?" He described the scene for us. "Roy talked Dean into taking off low and slow with a water ski harness attached to the plane. Dean took off too fast and yanked Roy airborne."

"On purpose," my father interrupted.

Birdman went on, "Feet dangling over the water, laughing like hell. Finally Roy had the sense enough to let go. Isaiah and I laughed so hard that Isaiah fell off the dock. Too drunk to swim. Then there were two fools in the drink to rescue. There's me out in the skiff, throwing out line to two men who didn't have sense to grab it." As he recalled that day I caught a glimpse of both men the way they used to be, carefree and young and alive.

"We didn't know what we were up against yet," Birdman said.

"That time I flew," my father recalled. A slight smile brushed across his face. "That was before I found Althea." He spoke of my mother as if he alone had discovered her, the same way we had discovered glass fishing floats half-buried in sand.

"It was better before," Birdman said.

My father ignored the remark. "When she comes back, we'll all sit on the dock together and plot like we used to in the old days," my father said. "Remember our old rule at sunset?"

"Mountain turns pink, time to drink," Birdman said.

"You got it. Things are different now that the loggers are coming. We can forget the old war between us. We need to stop them. We're stronger united than apart."

I watched them clink their glasses together, whiskey running down the sides and pooling onto the floor. Part of me resented how Birdman could slip under my father's spell so easily. Didn't he remember the stories I had brought to Floathouse Bay? But my mother and I had done the same, over and over, the forgetting coming easily when my father approached us with a smile and a promise.

When Sam and I were done packing it was close to night, too late to start out. Even my father knew that it was dangerous to walk in the dark. It was too easy to slip off a cliff, your foot hanging in empty air as you reached for branches that were too high to grab. It was too easy to walk up on a bear as it lay dozing and unafraid in its bed. We would start out at first light.

Birdman laid out a bedroll in the great room, stumbling a bit from the whiskey. Sam smiled at me briefly before disappearing toward the old clients' rooms downstairs, his old boathouse quarters abandoned now.

My father and I were left in a room that was still echoing with memories. I shifted from foot to foot, ready for flight.

"Something you should know. Your old room's been cleaned out," he said. "Burn barrel, mostly. Gave some things to Ernie to sell. Figured you took what you needed, and if you came back we could start over. You can sleep upstairs, in our old room. I can't manage the stairs, so I've been bunking down here. I don't sleep much these days anyway. Spend a lot of time out on the dock, just me and the sea, just thinking."

"What do you think about?" Regrets, I wondered, old stories? Was this where he would tell me what I needed to know?

"When you can't walk like you used to, there's plenty to think about, trust me. I think about the old men and Dean and me in Floathouse Bay, when we first came into this country, times that will never come again. I think about all the bays down the coast that I know better than I knew any living person. I think about everything."

I hesitated, thinking that this was the moment everything would become clear. My father would break in to a million pieces and tell me he was sorry for what he had done. He would say that he knew where my mother had gone and how to find her. That it was only a story they had made up to bring me home, and that everything had changed for the better, that things would be simple and sweet and good from now on. Both of them would turn into the parents that I suspected other people had, soft as old pillows.

That did not happen. Instead he turned his back on me and wheeled away; our conversation was over. I listened to his clumsy passage through the rooms, the wheels bumping into doorsills, unseen breakable things falling to the floor and shattering. I could tell where he was by the sounds he left in his wake. Some things hadn't changed at all.

Nine

It was true. Everything in my old room was gone. There was no sign that a girl named Winnie had ever lived here. The canopy bed my father had made for me was missing, perhaps broken up for firewood. The fairy tales that I had thumbed through until the pages fell apart no longer leaned in a drunken row along the windowsill. My collection of Japanese fishing floats, the schoolbooks, handmade wool sweaters, all vanished. The bare floor echoed with my steps. Shut up tight to save the heat, the room was cold and forlorn.

How could they have done this? I pictured my father with an ax, chopping up the bed and feeding it to the fire. My mother, coming down the stairs with an armful of books for the fish weir children. How long had they waited? Had they been fueled by anger or despair? Regret washed over me. I should have come sooner. I should never have left.

Then I remembered the hiding places, my mother and me in our nightgowns, our feet bare and our hair down as we waited out my father. I recalled the story of the little brother, a slippery fish to whom we would have to teach all the old lessons. There was the swing between rage and sorrow, fear and enchantment, an eternal pendulum. And finally the sweetness that lay within Floathouse Bay. I had been right to leave.

I closed the door against the past. The girl named Winnie who had slept here was long gone. She was never coming back. I walked down the hall and up toward my parents' old room, boards sighing under my feet.

My mother had always called this room the bird's nest. It was the only room on the third floor, reached by a short flight of spiraling stairs. My father had built it with windows on all four sides so when I stood inside I could see the slate-gray water of the bay and the mountains scraping the sky beyond. Buffeted by wind and close-growing spruce, it was almost as if I was perched high in the canopy of the forest, about to take flight.

There was still an indentation in the pillow where my mother had last laid her head. The flannel sheets were thrown back as though someone had just arisen. There were no clues to where she had gone. No letter, carefully centered on the nightstand. No empty hangers slowly turning on the closet rod. A glass rimmed with sticky residue—orange juice—still stood on the handmade wooden dresser. At any moment, it seemed, she would return.

I wrapped up in the old comforter and closed my eyes, but sleep wouldn't come. The house pulsed with the old noises. As the leaves whispered, tree branches slowly and insistently scraped across the windows. The gentle rundown of the generator as Sam or my father clicked it off for the night. The sturdy hum of the gas refrigerator. But there were sounds that were missing. The bass of the clients' snores from under the floorboards. The tiny, guilty, scurrying steps of their wives as they moused around the kitchen with the lights off, pinching off pieces of brownie after insisting on eating only salads for dinner. The low music of my parents' voices on a good day, the square of light showing from under their bedroom door late, so late.

I whispered to myself the rules that had always worked, boundaries that made me feel safe in a place that was not always safe.

Never turn your back on the ocean.
Only harvest shellfish in months with an r.
Don't run from a bear.
Never turn a boat broadside in a following sea.
Hold on to copperbush when climbing slippery slopes.
Follow the deer trails; they know the best way.
Never leave harbor on a Friday.
No bananas onboard a boat or hats on a bed.
Don't whistle at sea; you will whistle up a storm.

When I was little I whispered those rules every night, over and over until I fell asleep. If I forgot one, I went back and started over. There had been a comfort in them, a promise that if I followed each one, life would be even and unchanging. This time the rules did not work. I got up, pulling on my mother's fleece jacket from the closet.

The path down to the ocean was lit by a tentative moon, floating in and out of dark clouds. My father was sitting next to the dock, his back against it, a bottle between his knees. His chair sat on the dock and he had somehow gotten himself down to the beach, a ten-foot drop.

He had not seen me yet, and I suddenly remembered being seven years old and asking my mother questions she could not answer. Why the salmon came back to the same stream, when they had no map to follow. Out of the whole big ocean, why this one tiny stream, I asked. What was so special about this one, when there were thousands of others?

My mother was filleting fish and only half listening. Her knife cleanly separated delicate spine from meat, the filmy white bones from the pieces that were good. She threw what she did not want into the ocean for the sea lions to fight over.

My job was to pack the fish in the big white cooler with wheels so that we could move it over to the workbench next to the tall freezer in the shed. Then we would vacuum seal the fillets into bags and let them slowly freeze into rock-hard lumps. The fillets were slippery, the flesh cold rubber. They were hard to hold onto.

My mother set down her bloody gloves and looked at me. "The salmon have their own map," she said.

My father heard us from where he sat, baiting up a halibut skate with some of the discards. The long hooks on the line were curved and sharp. When he was done he would row out into the bay and set the skate deep into the water, the line spooling out far, farther than I could see, a pale white line falling through to the place where the water turned black. He would attach an orange buoy to the top of the skate and row back to us.

"A map? Like ours?" I had thought of our charts, almost as wide as I was tall, sheets of blue and gold where the land was not important, just the sea. My father had shown me our own bay on the charts, moving his finger over the places where the shallows were, where the hidden rock shelf lurked, the other places where it was deep, too deep to anchor. The charts are not perfect, he always said. That is why you have to watch, every time. Do not trust anything, ever.

"Their map is in their heads," my mother said. "The salmon stay out in the ocean for two years, more sometimes. They circle far out there, farther than you can swim. But when it is time to go back, they can find their own stream in this big ocean by what they remember."

She was finished. She stepped out of her bibs and hung them on a hook by the boathouse. Her hair was knotted behind her head. A streak of blood smudged her forehead. She trudged back up the dock.

"You should tell her the truth once in a while," my father had said, loud enough for my mother to hear. "Nobody really knows the answer about the salmon. It's all just a guess."

She did not turn around, just kept walking up the path.

He stood up and jumped down into the skiff, the boat rocking beneath him. Like always he kept his balance, shifting between each foot. "The salmon come back, Winnie," he said, pulling on the oars. "That's all we really need to know."

In seconds he was gone, moving past the island where we had once found remains of a trapper's cabin; so far out in the bay that he was nearly invisible. I squinted, trying to turn him back into a man.

Years later, I was back on the same beach. Out to sea, past the cluster of islands, the ocean looked calm. There were no hints of the currents that raged below its surface. Nothing revealed the jagged teeth of rocks that did not show up on the charts. The water looked serene, unruffled, safe. But I knew differently. There was so much hidden beneath.

"Get me some big rocks, won't you, Winnie?" he asked, looking up and seeing me.

"What do you need rocks for?" I asked, but I had never refused him. My fingers closed around a stone still damp from the sea and I brought it back by his feet to join a pile he had already started. It was a small cairn, the kind hunters made to find their way back from the uplands. He ignored me, hunching over something.

I realized what he was doing. He was building a fire on the beach. We had done this often in the fall when the chill set in but the twilight lingered long and nobody could sleep. We had been just past the manic days of summer, the fishing clients hitting the water early, and the sun barely setting. We turned feral then, sleeping only in quick snatches with quilts hung over the windows to block out the light.

In fall, though, we felt the hint of what was to come. The days slowed with each passing twilight. There was time between clients. We even moved slower with each minute of lost daylight. Our blood seemed to thicken. Fall was a time sandwiched between the glorious run of summer and the blank white slate of winter ahead.

We had built beach fires low enough on the stones near the water's edge so that the higher tides of the season would wash up and smother the flames long after we had gone to bed. My father liked to sit out here listening to the crackle of the flames and the murmur of the ocean. Once he told me that it sounded to him like the land and sea were talking like old friends and that if he listened hard enough he could make out what they were saying. Once he told me that this was the only time that his mind stood still.

I watched him. He opened a Crown Royal bag and spread out the contents. First there were amber balls of pitch, set carefully below crumbling bark from the underbellies of fallen trees. Then he took out his knife and shaved away curls of wood from a handful of twigs. Finally he sprinkled wisps of lichen over the top and lit it.

He hunched over the small pile, blowing steadily.

I had watched him build many fires. He had a knack for starting a fire in the rain, or the snow, or the wind. Either you're born with it or you're not, he used to say. He had the patience to wait instead of barging in, to rock back on his heels and contemplate while the fire took its time. That was the trick, the waiting.

A thin tendril of smoke curled up from the pile. A small flame wormed through the lichen. My father grinned.

"Still got it," he said.

I hovered on my heels, unable to commit to leaving or staying. Covertly I studied his face. I recognized this mood, a step down toward despair, a mood my mother had always hated but that I always kind of liked. In this one he was thoughtful, his words carefully chosen, each one a polished stone falling from his mouth. In this one he was reachable, a spark of recognition lighting between us.

He had lost the wool hat somewhere and his hair, all white now, spiraled over his head in disarray. He was smaller than he had been years ago, and his glass eye gleamed in the firelight, but otherwise he could have been the same man he used to be.

"I miss it," he said, startling me. "I miss the way things used to be." He pulled his jacket tighter around himself. "Sometimes, out on the ocean, in the boat, I felt like I was riding the back of some sleeping animal, rolling as it dreamed," he said. "I'd look out at the gray backs of the swells, all speckled with kelp, you remember. And I'd just wonder. Wonder at all sorts of things. Where the waves came from that passed under the boat. What was swimming below me in two hundred feet of water. What would happen if I swam down as deep as I could without ever coming up for air."

I swallowed hard. "The way it used to be wasn't very good. Don't you remember?"

He didn't answer for a minute, poking at the fire with a stick. Then he said, "I cheated death a hundred times on that ocean. It takes you and grinds you up and spits you out. But it's so beautiful, so mysterious. That's what kept me going back."

He held the stick and we both looked at it. It had caught a spark and was beginning to burn.

"We came back from the hunt early and you were gone," he told me. "Weather was closing in. The client was in a rage. Why can't we just hunt Never Summer, he kept asking. There are plenty of bears here. It was arbitrary not to, he said, he paid plenty for the hunt, and he was going to sue. Go ahead, I told him. We don't hunt the bears in Never Summer.

"Sam offered to go and get you. You had gone to Floathouse Bay; we all knew it. Where else would you go? I told him that you were a woman, old enough to know your own mind. If you wanted to come back, you would. You had your own reasons for staying gone."

"What did she say?"

"She always said you would come back. That you had promised her you would."

But I had never promised that. Had I? There had been so many promises. It was easier to only remember the pull of the cord, my mother turning to look as I steered the Lund away from the dock. There had been a moment when I had thought she would run toward me. There had been a moment when the boat was not too far away for her to step in. That moment passed. She only stood there, watching me leave.

In the beginning I had meant to turn back, perhaps only go as far as the red cliffs. I had meant to show her that I could leave, that I was not afraid. But the farther I went from the dock, the easier it was to point the boat straight ahead. After all, you never turned a boat broadside in a following sea.

"She wanted to name you something different," my father was saying. "Something light. Fluffy. I said no, that a woman out here needed something heavy to carry with her. Something with heft to it. She could name the next one, I told her. Trouble was, there never was a next one. She never could make a baby stick except for you."

If I spoke now he might stop talking. I had seen it before, a sudden clamming up, a brisk dismissal. I sat very still.

"She lost a couple of babies up at Lookout Point," he said. "Early enough that she didn't need a hospital, though. They weren't even really babies, small as little fish. She said maybe they would come back as salmon someday and swim their way home."

There were no babies. There was my answer. Had she ever wished for that so hard that she believed it was true?

"You'll find her," my father said. "You have to find her." His hair blew around his face. The fire flickered.

"You know that she may have left for a reason," I said, choosing my words with care. "Even if all she went to was the lake. She must have known that you couldn't follow her that far. You must know that maybe she doesn't want you to find her."

"That's not true," he said quickly. "She had no reason to leave. Although perhaps I had a bit of a heavy hand at times. In the past," he added quickly. "Before." His hand indicated the chair.

I couldn't stop myself. "A heavy hand? Is that what you call it?"

"There were no broken bones," he said. "I wasn't that kind of man."

"But you hurt her. I saw it. I saw all of it. She showed me what you did." I saw another ghost of the old anger in his face and I shrank back just a little. Then I remembered the bruises around my mother's wrist like a bracelet. My mother's hand, a washcloth in her fist. Her voice, making excuses. It was an accident. He works so hard for us, out in all kinds of weather, his hands splitting from saltwater, his body twisting from early arthritis. I make it happen, my mother would say. It is always me who starts it. Don't start it, I would howl, but my mother shushed me by turning on the tap, the water so hot it curled my toes. What would we do without him, she would say, not a question but a statement, difficult to refute.

My father said, "I don't know what you think you remember. It was a long time ago. But we were happy. Everything was perfect. Until last year, the cruisers. The helicopter. They are going to ruin it for us. For us and the bears."

"But that's not the way it was. That's not what happened."

"It was, for me," he said. "It was perfect, until the accident. It changed everything."

I could not speak, a deep flush of anger rolling over me. How could he say that? Didn't he remember?

"Winnie, you were young then. You misunderstood things."

I scrambled to my feet, kicking at the pile of rocks he had collected, wanting to hurt him. The cairn toppled, rocks scattering. One rolled onto my foot, a brief jolt of pain. I shook it free.

"She told me everything," I said. "Everything."

My father drank deeply from the bottle. He coughed. "No," he said. "Not everything." He winced as he tried to straighten his legs. "First time I saw her in the Hell and Gone, she reminded me of a little bird, unable to fly. A bird that had lost her wings. They do that, you know, if they've lived on islands long enough. Forget how to fly.

"Curled up in the corner, fishermen circling like vultures, no money, no way out. Her skin was so pale I could see blue veins through it. You're coming with me, I said, took her hand. She came with me, I didn't make her come. She would never leave me. Not in a million years."

I thought of what Isaiah had said. "Did she ever tell you about where she came from?"

He set the bottle carefully beside him, the liquid glowing in the light of the fire. "She followed some loser who brought her to Alaska, the same type of guy who comes up here every summer, going to live off the land with a handful of matches and an ax. Bag of rice, maybe, if he was one of the smarter ones. He ditched her once he got the offer from the pipeline, realized easy money was better than squatting in some waterless cabin at forty below or living in a canvas wall tent. Didn't want anyone to tie him down, just left her flat, jumped on a plane. The day I walked into the Hell and Gone and got her, that was the best decision I ever made. Dean said I had gone off the deep end of the ocean, letting someone wrap herself around me like that. He hated it that she chose me. Thought she would pick him, the women always had. Plenty of fish in the sea and birds in the air, he said. Can't you go find yourself another one and let me have her, he asked." He laughed, but it had a bitter undertone.

This was the same thing that Isaiah had said, but as I thought back through the years I only saw the handing over of a cup of tea, a casual glance. There had been nothing to indicate anything smoldering in Uncle Dean. If anything, he had been the kind of person trouble ran off of like water on a coat. Never able to sit still, he bounced on his toes as he waited for storms to pass.

What else had I missed?

Above us, the clouds thickened into soup, any clearing long gone to the east. "Rain, maybe, before long," my father said. "Winchester, your mother is like a puzzle. She will give you one piece, and then another, when she feels like it, and it can take a lifetime to put them together. I didn't ask her what she wasn't willing to tell me. I liked how there was always more to know, and I figured if I waited long enough, I would learn it all."

The light left his one good eye and it became blank and opaque, matching the other. If I didn't know better I would have said he had begun to cry.

Impossible. My father hardly ever cried.

"Do you think it's true, Winnie? Do you think she's really left me?"

Words tumbled from my mouth before I could stop them. "Why were you always so angry? Did you know that I used to think that was how everyone was? But Isaiah and Birdman aren't that way. I don't think Sam is that way. Maybe that's why she left. She got tired of the angry."

The words hung in the air, impossible to take back. I had never spoken to my father like this. What had I done? I stood there, my hand to my mouth. He sat silent for a minute, looking away from me and out to the ocean. I expected a flash of anger, but he seemed thoughtful instead. "I came to Alaska when I was seventeen. My father said he would sign the paper to spring me from school early if I took Dean with me. Thought Dean would keep me out of trouble," he said. "I had an itch to be someone other than Dean's kid brother, and still I couldn't get away from him. You need me, he said, to fly the plane, and he was right. I didn't think he would last up here. I wanted to make it hard for him so that I could shine for once. But I needed him up here. This coast was like nothing I had ever seen before. You can't be soft here, Winchester. Alaska takes people like that and chews them up. You've got to be like stone, not like water."

"You went too far toward the stone," I whispered, softly enough that my words might be covered by the sound of water.

He threw the stick back into the fire. I couldn't tell if he heard me. A sliver of moonlight played across his face, a sucker hole in the clouds passing by.

"I saw that she wrote you a letter. Saw her taking it down to the barge. Told you what I asked her to do, I guess. Because what's the point, a beat-up old man, can't fight anymore. Too hard to sit here and be punched in the gut, roads built, trees cut, no way to stop them."

"She couldn't do what you asked. She loves you too much."

"I suppose you are right." He peered at me. "Don't get that look on your face. I wasn't going to ask you, either. A man's got to do his own living and dying. Took me awhile to come to that conclusion, but I finally got there."

Grateful for the night that partially shaded my face, I sat down. There was a question I had been waiting to ask. I thought that now, in the dark, he might answer.

"Tell me. What really happened in Enchantment Bay? I need to know."

"Winnie, you've got know that it was a rookie mistake. Should never have set foot in that bay. Don't ask unless you really want to know."

Did I want to know? Something had happened, something that nobody wanted to talk about. I could feel the weight of it, and I suddenly felt too young for all of this. I wanted to find one of our old hiding places, but there was nowhere left to hide.

"Sam might tell you. It's really his story to tell."

"Sam was there?"

"He was there."

"Why didn't he stop it?"

My father laughed, a short bark in the darkness. "I told you already, ask him."

I shook my head and buried my hands deeper into my borrowed

jacket. It still smelled like my mother, an indefinable scent of glycerin soap and the peppermint oil she used to soothe her cracked hands. It seemed that she was still here, close enough to touch.

I asked the question that had always needled at me whenever I watched the bears in the streams. Their powerful muscles bunched under their skin, their claws longer than my fingers. Didn't they know how much stronger they were than any of us?

"At least tell me what it was like."

He was quiet for a minute, gathering rocks and rebuilding the mound. Then he said, "There was an absence of pain. Your body protects you, you know. You go into a place almost like dreaming. There was no pain until later."

He rolled a rock between his fingers before adding it to the pile. The cairn tilted under the weight of the stones.

"I've been close to bears, close enough to feel their breath on my face. I've led a hundred men to kill shots. Maybe this was the way the bears decided to settle the score."

I let my mind linger on how it must have been. There would be the crunch of breaking bones, the snap of branches as they rolled in their strange embrace. Growls and screams would be interwoven along with the breaths of both combatants. It was all too terrible to contemplate, even as a thought wormed its way in. *Now you know. You understand the sudden betrayal of a blow in the night.*

"That's all I want to tell you. Ask Sam if you want to know the rest."

When I said nothing, he went on. "Here's the thing you need to know about Sam. He's not tough, not the way we are, you and me. This country scares him to the bones. It's too big for some people, and it's too big for him. He doesn't really know how to move through it except by following someone strong. If he's got that, he can go forever. When you go up the red cliffs, you have to be strong enough for the both of you. Birdman I'm not worried about. He'd survive anything; he's been to hell and back already. But you're my daughter and you should know this. Understand?"

My father hoisted himself up to the dock. For a moment he stood suspended between the chair and the ground, almost the man he used to be. Then he slumped down, his shoulders rounded. "Go on now, Winnie. I've got things to think about."

It felt wrong to leave him out there on the dock, a little fire burning on the beach, soon to be swallowed by the tide. I wavered for a moment. He had never been so honest with me, and I thought that the night might bring more answers. But my father had already forgotten me, his head dipping low on his chest. I thought that he might be sleeping or that he might need help wheeling back up the broken dock to the lodge.

But as I waited, it was clear that he did not need me. He needed none of us. He wanted instead to wrap himself up in half-truths like a tattered blanket. The chart he had drawn for himself, a vague map of what our lives had been, was not the same one I remembered. In the end I slipped away, leaving him to the fire and the sea.

Ten

Upstairs in the bird's nest, the night ticked by one interminable second at a time. I lay under my mother's comforter fully dressed, ready for escape.

Never leave harbor on a Friday.

Only harvest shellfish . . .

It occurred to me that there had been other unspoken rules in our bay. Never trust what someone tells you, even if they look you straight in the eyes. What they remember is not the truth that you know.

Dawn came reluctantly, a shy girl late for the dance. It touched the highest peaks with a shell-pink blush, slowly creeping down toward our bay and settling with an almost audible sigh on the water. The red cliffs held darkness the longest because of the way they leaned in toward the ocean. On some winter days the sun never reached parts of the cliffs at all.

It would be hours yet.

I turned the pillow to find a cool side. It was flat from age, and as I punched it down a few feathers escaped from an unseen hole and floated lazily toward the floor. Something else did, too.

I reached down and grabbed it. A small piece of paper torn from a logbook of some kind, it looked like it had been folded a hundred times. Something was scribbled on it in pencil, but time had erased some of the letters. I sat cross-legged, puzzling it out.

I'll never forget the night of the fog. If you change your mind, you know where to find me.

What did this mean? Was it the beginning of a story she had meant to tell me? There had been many nights when the fog rolled in from the ocean, rolling over us in a suffocating wall of white. It was impossible to pick out one night in all the nights of fog there had been. I crumpled the paper and shoved it into my mother's jacket pocket. I would throw it away in the morning. Whatever secrets those words held, they had no relevance now.

Sleep remained elusive, just out of my reach. I imagined that everyone else in the world slept but me. Isaiah snored in his float-house room, wondering what had become of us and when we would return. Ernie and his wife lay tangled in their town sheets, our stories filling their dreams. Up and down the coast, all the others I had never met slept too, their lives surely much less complicated and troubled than ours. Sam and Birdman catnapped downstairs, their dreams unknown to me.

By now my father must have wheeled back into the house and shoehorned himself between whichever walls he had chosen. Perhaps pain kept him sleepless. And my mother, did she sleep? Did she lie awake like I did, searching through the shadowy past?

I floated in the middle of sleep, waking as the early morning hours wore on, and was startled awake by the sound of desperate footsteps hitting the stairs. Sam burst through the door, looming over me, his coat buttoned wrong, his hair a wild mop. He had misplaced his glasses somewhere and squinted at me in the darkness. "Winnie. I went out early to check the boat. Something's happened. Something's gone wrong."

He paced the room as I scrambled out of bed and pulled on my boots. "What's happened? Has she come home?"

"No. No, she hasn't come home, but something is wrong out at the dock. Hurry, here's your coat, come on!"

We ran together out of the house, down the slippery boardwalk and out onto the dock. At first I saw nothing unusual. The sky was overcast, an edge to the air that spoke of winter's unwillingness to let go. The air was swollen with rain, and looking at the dock I could tell it had already rained once and had stopped a while ago. Recently by the looks of it. I could see where we had come, clear wet outlines of our boots.

I could see something else.

The parallel lines of a wheelchair, rolling straight out to the end of the dock.

No. No.

"It's too late," Sam said. "Even if we dove now. An hour, maybe two. Maybe more."

"The rocks," I said. "He was gathering rocks on the beach." Rocks he had taken with him to the bottom of the ocean. It was obvious what he had done. Rocks in his pockets. Big ones, so he could sink faster and stay down longer. Long enough to run out of air.

Surely it wasn't true. Surely my father was here, playing a trick on us. Hiding in the trees. In the remains of the boat shed. He would come out any second now, grinning at our concern. "Cheated death once again," he would say. Surely if he were gone the world would feel shrunken somehow. Instead everything was the same. The whisper of waves. The voice of the sea.

The fire was dead out. The pile of rocks was gone.

He wasn't anywhere.

"We need to dive. To be sure." Maybe there was a chance. He might have just done it, still on his last breath. I would dive down in a cloud of bubbles and bring him back up on my back. He hadn't meant to do it. Maybe his chair had gotten too close. There had been a moment of free fall. Accident. *Rookie mistake.*

But the rocks. There was no mistaking the rocks.

"This isn't an abalone free dive," Sam said. "We would need tanks. You know what the current does around here."

He was right.

There was nothing we could do.

I walked to the end of the dock on legs that barely held me. I looked in.

Part of me was afraid I would see him, his hair tangled in seaweed, his eyes open as he floated. But the water was calm and deep. There was no hint of what lay beneath. *Swim down as deep as I could.*

My mother and I knew how to swim. My father had insisted on it, but we never stayed in the water long. In fifteen minutes the water would turn the blood in your veins to sludge. In fifteen minutes your breath would freeze in your lungs. In fifteen minutes you would be dead.

"He must have thought she was really gone," Sam said. He sank to his knees, his fingers tracing the wheel marks, receding now. Pretty soon they would vanish as the day marched on, oblivious.

"Roy Hudson. Hard to believe he took this route," Birdman said. He had come up behind us and was staring into the water, hands shoved into the pockets of his army coat. "Sat on this dock, all five of us dipping our toes in, daring each other to jump in all the way. Only Roy and Dean would. We all drank whiskey like water, just like we did last night. Talked about all the things we would do. Climb all the mountains, sail the whole ocean. No limits. Now only two of us are left."

"Three," I whispered. "Three are left."

"I hope you are right," he said. "But you have to be prepared for the other."

I held back the burning itch of tears because this did not seem real. It was instead a story my mother had made up. *What if,* she would say. *What if a waterspout spun into the bay and lifted us up into its mouth? We could land anywhere. Kansas. Kentucky. Canada. What would we do then?*

What if my father disappeared into the sea? What then?

We told stories of my father, the three of us huddled against the raw wind. That was what he would have liked, stories through which he walked large. He was always the star of his show whether he truly had been or not. The snow got deeper, the bears larger, the sea wilder, facts moved like puzzle pieces until they fit his idea of what should have been. After a while I thought that he believed them too.

Even though I knew what the others did not, I stared at the bay, wondering. Had he really wanted this? Had he realized, too late, that the wheels would not stop on the slippery dock? Moss was so quick to cover wood unless you kept after it with scrapers and chemicals. Or, I thought with a shiver, maybe pushed? My mother, finally keeping her promise? But there were no footprints, only wheels.

The bay held no answers. It was as cold and serene as it ever was.

"Knots always held for him," Sam said. "Boats always ran. Never got high and dry on the beach or had to swim for the anchor. He understood this country in a way I always wanted to but never could."

"Either you get it or you don't," Birdman agreed. "Rest of us spend our lives worrying at it, chewing off a bit at a time. Others, like Roy, take big bites and somehow get away with it."

"Outran avalanches, pushed through ocean swells, got away with anchoring in a sandy bottom," Sam agreed. "None of the rest of us could ever get away with what he did."

He had always known the power of the sea. He would have known how short fifteen minutes was. And how long it was, too.

"The Hudson boys," Birdman said. "Both of them gone now. End of an era."

"What happens next?" Sam asked. None of us answered. Over our heads a pair of scrappy ravens worried a lone eagle not caring or not aware that the larger bird could kill them with a slash of its talons. The three of them swooped and dove in a strange ballet.

"Dean was first," Birdman said. "He went to a place that none of us could follow. I've seen plenty of people disappear, but that one hit everyone on the coast hard. Everyone loved Dean. Everyone thought he was their best friend."

"I remember how he was after Uncle Dean disappeared. It took three days for him to get up and start the boats again. I remember liking it, how my mother and I eddied around like he was a rock in a creek, as if for once he didn't matter so much to us. But she didn't like it so much. She said she missed the fire in his eyes."

What I didn't say was what she had told me years later: "Don't fall for someone like Sam. He's boring, but sweet. Like angel food cake. No spice." She had hugged me tight. "Fall for someone a little bit crazy," she said. "Promise me."

"Why do you think he flew that day?" I asked Birdman, the only person who might know.

"Why would anyone fly in that lousy weather, we all thought later. Ernie saw him down on the float docks all suited up to go. He had made it back from your place with a bunch of clients with him, all clueless and spitting Copenhagen. Still had one load to go. None of the rest of the pilots were flying. Boats all stayed at the dock. There was no reason in hell good enough to be out there. Ernie said that he had barely made it back in the barge, twenty-foot seas, and Dean should stay on the beach. But Dean just grinned and said he knew he could make it. Said the sky was calling his name. If anyone could have made it, Dean Hudson would have."

"He looked for days," I said. "Even after the searchers had all given up and gone home." I never knew where my father had gone in those dark days after Dean's disappearance. He did not ask us to go with him. I pictured him alone in an open boat, puttering from island to coast and back again, both hoping and fearing what he might find.

"We looked for Dean too," Birdman said. "Even though it was after the trouble and Roy would never have asked us for help. We circled out there for days in the skiff. Sometimes we still look. The ocean gives up things sometimes, like airplane floats. The land never does."

"I like the ocean," Sam said. "You read the charts; you know what you are getting. Even if the charts miss something, there are plenty of stories. Generations worth of stories, so you always know which places to stay away from. You don't have that on land." He tossed a rock into the water, and it made a circle of rings that lasted for a long time.

"I only felt safe on land with Roy there beside me. 'You'll never make a good guide,' he used to tell me, because I hung so close to him. You have to strike off with a compass on your own, he would tell me. Get lost. Make some mistakes. If you don't have the guts to do that, you'll never get it right. He was right about that. I never got it the way he did. The way he moved through both land and sea like it wasn't separate from him, that was something I never figured out how to do."

I realized that most of my father's stories had been about the sea. He told us about the bay where moon jellyfish gathered so thickly that the water boiled white. About the deer he saw in the middle of channels, swimming miles from shore. The slurp of water across the bow, the stars clustered like coals across the night robe of the sky. The time that the anchor dragged free, deep in the night, and he found himself floating in the boat far from land, as if there was no land, only a deep, deep ocean for as far as the world went. It was when you got to shore that you were in trouble. There were so many ways that the land was more dangerous than the sea. Falls off cliffs, fast-running rivers, bears, and everything else that waited there.

I never quite believed that. You couldn't breathe in the sea. Boats could sink. Tsunamis could slither across the middle of the ocean, caused by earthquakes in far-off Japan. But my father thought he could dance over the sea untouched by any calamity. I knew that my mother believed that about him too.

"One time," Sam remembered, "the first season, we were anchored out in the Maze, and Roy told me to take us home. Hell, I didn't know where we were, all those islands look the same. Bunch of dead ends, shallow sandbars, little keyholes. I had no clue which way to go. Roy looked at me like I was a couple pieces of bread short of a sandwich. No big thing, he said. Just go back the same way we came, he said. Like it was that simple. He had the whole coastline there in his head. Never even needed a map."

The wind ruffled the ocean like a lover's touch. A raft of sea otters lounged on their backs riding the swell and nibbling on sea urchins. Gulls dotted the water, waiting out the tide change. The ravens and the eagle flew on to another bay to continue their battle. The rain brought out the silver-tongued waterfalls, dozens of them, falling in unimpeded shining arcs into the sea. It seemed strange that everything should look the same, as though it were an ordinary day. Instead it should be one of the times when thirty-knot winds tumbled over the divide, bending the trees nearly in two, flags of snow blowing off the mountains, the sea whipped into a frenzy of snarling white.

We would climb the cliffs anyway. What else could we do? With full packs, we turned our backs on the ocean. Walking slowly we climbed from the beach fringe, taking the old path to the muskeg above. Years ago my father had laced a rope through the trees so that we could walk up the steepest part while holding onto it for balance. I tested it and it still held, although it had frayed at the edges and turned white with age. I wondered how long it would be here. How long would the lodge that my father built still stand before a tree crashed into it, the roof caved, the otters moved in? How long would it take to erase him from the world?

Coming out of the trees, I stopped at the place that we always called Lookout Point. Like the prow of a ship, the point jutted out over the ocean, a mossy headland about to set sail. Deep green seawater foamed around the base of the cliffs a hundred feet below.

I remembered James Tucker's grave, somewhere under my feet. Unlike James, my father would never have a grave. Instead, his bones would tumble along the bottom of the ocean. With time and enough storms, they could roll right out of the bay and into Turn Back Strait, where the current would carry them faster than a person could run. Shards of bone could wash up years later on the Trader Islands, mingled with the blue wink of beach grass and thousands of crushed shells. He was really and truly gone.

I hunted around where I remembered the gravestone to be but could find no trace of James Tucker's grave. Maybe it had finally mossed over, tendrils of fine green plants lacing together to cover it completely and for good.

I remembered our stories about James and his fate. Suddenly I was unsure. What had been real? *You misunderstood things*. Had I made this up? But no, I remembered it, the flat coolness of the stone. Didn't I?

I wandered to the farthest point of the headland, wanting to be away from the others. The line between truth and fiction seemed a thin one. Standing there I could see what I had always believed as truth: the curve of the never-changing land as it bent away toward the horizon, sturdy and firm. It looked exactly as I had remembered it. But I knew even that was deceiving. Forces were working at it, chewing it away. Wind, water, tide, snow. Even though it looked the same to me now, the land on which I stood had changed imperceptibly. In ten years, twenty, it would change again.

"Where are you?" I whispered. The branches on the stunted trees shivered in the wind. There was no answer.

I looked back down to the bay, spotting the dock like a pale finger stretching out into the water. I imagined a man in a wheelchair, carefully gathering rocks from a beach. Placing them in the pockets of his wool jacket. One last gulp of liquid courage. Fire in his belly. Rolling to the end of the dock. Looking around for the last time. Taking a breath. The splash. The silence. The fire still burning on the beach.

I swallowed down a lump in my throat. "Winnie," Sam called. "What do you see?"

I looked again for the headstone. Sam had never come up here. He had never seen the gravestone. This was a memory only my mother and I shared.

"Nothing," I said, and it was true.

I turned away from the sea. Ahead all I could see was a thick cedar forest. The trees here were survivors of a war zone, battling gale winds that swept off the gulf, thick cloud bands of rain that drove into their bark with the force of bullets. It was hard not to admire the trees' tenacity. These were not dying, not yet. They clung to a slope washed by water, landslides and avalanches a constant threat. "We want to head northwest, through the cedars," Birdman said. "Look to your compass, try to keep a straight line. We'll get to the backside of the red cliffs in just about a mile."

The cedar forest was mostly why my mother and I always turned around at the muskeg; that, and my father's command not to go farther. There was no light ahead, any available space taken up by twisted branches. This was silent and fierce combat, each tree stubbornly refusing to concede space to its neighbor. I hesitated.

There seemed to be no way to move through.

Birdman, just about to disappear inside the belly of the forest, looked back and saw me pause.

"Winnie, dear," he said, "in the wilderness, sooner or later, you have to do something even if it's wrong. Second thoughts will kill you."

I took a deep breath and plunged in.

It was only a mile by map, but it took the better part of a day. The three of us were swallowed up by the cedar forest, a mass of limbs and trunks as solid as rock. The trees grew so thick and close that I had to slip out of my pack and turn sideways to pass through. The spiky needles scraped over my face and arms as if warning me to stay out. They pulled my hair and knocked me down. I was caught in a web of branches and trees so thick that I could not remember which way the sky was. I kept a firm grip on my compass, staring at the slender needle as if it were my only chance for survival.

Most times it was more like swimming than walking. The others passed somewhere parallel to me, perhaps close enough to touch but not to see. Our calls echoed through the forest as we moved through, my feet sometimes not touching the ground as I balanced on a tightly woven mat of branches.

After an unknown amount of time I came upon Sam, resting on a fallen trunk. His coat hung off one shoulder and a long pink scratch ran down his face. I sat down beside him, resting against the shaggy bark. We gulped down stale water from our canteens and took inventory of the route ahead.

It was dark. Nothing lived in the cedars. Even the deer had forsaken this place.

I could not imagine my mother, alone, slipping through these trees. Why would anyone come this way? I could tell Sam was thinking the same thing. "Should we go back?" I asked. Doubt circled in my head like birds. "Maybe she walked the coast. Flagged down a boat. She could be halfway to Juneau by now."

"That never works," Sam said. "The boats don't get that close because of the rocks. You know how hard it is to see someone on shore? I've had a hell of a time just in one bay trying to find the clients after a stalk sometimes."

He shrugged his coat back on. "I thought about it the first year. Just quitting this place for good. Hiking out to the red cliffs and waving down a long-liner. Leaving you all high and dry."

"I never knew," I whispered. Sam had not been one of us. He never joined us in the evenings when the clients sprawled large and loose limbed on the sofas, their boots propped on the coffee table. The bottles emptied and the voices getting louder, Sam had faded away to his room above the boathouse. Assistant guides were a rung lower than everyone else, and nobody invited him to stay either except for an occasional client's wife, tipsy on fresh air and white wine. None of us, especially Sam, took those offers seriously. The wives were like frosting on a cake, fluffy pretty things, but not important.

On the afternoons we had stood side by side with fillet knives, I thought that I knew him, but now I realized that he listened to me talk about whales and salmon and everything else I thought I knew, but I had never thought to ask. Caught in my own world, I never even wondered about his.

"You have to know this about me, Winnie. I'm not an educated guy. Barely made it through high school, D grades all the way, and nobody thought I would amount to much. Where I'm from, a guy either went for the sugar beet factory or the marines. Had a bunch of kids, held down a stool at the local pub, and called it good. Kind of felt like drowning to me. I could tell that Roy was waiting for me to give up like all of the other guides before me. That's what kept me from walking the coast. Damn it, I was going to prove him wrong.

But every day I woke up with a knot in my stomach. There's so many ways to get it wrong out here."

I knew what he meant. There was a thin line between life and death. I imagined it to be much thicker in other places, where the land's belly was flat and safe and warm instead of cloaked in greasy deer cabbage and puncturing devil's club. There were places where you could wear shorts and sandals all day long and tan your skin to a golden bronze. I was used to the way it was here; I knew nothing else. But Sam, coming from somewhere soft, would not be.

"I've been everywhere, it seems like," he said. "Tried my hand at a bunch of different things. Walked steel. Drove truck. Fought fire. I always quit them, thinking there was something better, something fresher. Know what I mean? Guess you don't. People like you, you're glued to a place and can't imagine leaving it. There were all those little towns I drove though—Alpine, Texas; Baker, Nevada—just dots on a map, lights on in the houses, and I'd get this kind of lonely feeling as I went through, like I envied them on one hand but thought I was the luckiest guy in the world on the other because I could keep on driving. It got old, you know? I just kept on looking to find that place that said home to me. Where I could stop moving. Sometimes I thought I had left it too long, that I'd be some old guy driving forever. When I saw that newspaper ad Roy put in the paper, I was couch surfing in Seattle, waiting for my luck to turn, down to my last hundred dollars. It was a lifesaver, I thought. Do you remember the day I showed up?"

I did remember. I was fifteen, poised on an invisible brink between child and woman. We had gone out to meet the plane, stuffed with clients and enormous duffel bags. Sam climbed out last, a fringe of blond hair a little too long, his eyes brimming with excitement. Looking at him, I had felt a little fizz of possibility.

"Miles and miles of mountains," Sam recalled. "We flew straight over the island and all I could see were lakes still frozen, rivers so big that nobody could cross them. Places where people have never set foot. Then we fly into this little bay, taking that downwind turn sharp, and land on the water, and there you three are, like people from another world. Rifles over your shoulders, all three of you, like you were defending the place, I didn't know then that was how you did it on the coast. Nothing domesticated about any of you three. I had never seen a girl before who looked like you, hair almost silver, eyes blue but with ice in them like the lakes we had flown over. You looked like you had grown out of this place. This is it, I told myself. This is where it will all work out for me.

"Now Roy's gone and it just feels like I'm adrift in the ocean. What will we do without him?"

I knew so much about my father that Sam did not. He had seen only what he wanted to see—a volatile and vibrant man, leaning out over the bow of a boat, binoculars in one hand. But Sam was right. Despite what I knew as the truth, there was still an unbridgeable gap that my father had used to fill with his presence. Never Summer Bay had been so much about him that he and the bay had often seemed to be one thing. Now it would be an entirely different place.

"Back home," Sam said, "the same guys on the same bar stools. They can't even switch it up, move to a different seat. Slap me on the back, buy me a round, say things like they wish they could go out west, start over. You can, I tell them, you just need a set of keys and a map, but they just say they can't. Mortgage, wife, got to pay for the boat and the ATV. And then I wonder, what the hell made me different, why that life is enough for them and not enough for me."

"What about your parents?" I asked. "What are they like?"

Sam palmed his water bottle. "My father, he likes to say that he's never spent a night outside of his house in twenty years. Slept in the same bed for twenty years, he says. Kissed only one woman, owned the same set of wheels. He goes three places: the bowling alley, the gas station to bitch over coffee with the other laid-off factory guys, and to the grain store to buy new Carhartts. He and my mom, they just don't dream very big. They think I'll be back. Everybody thinks I'll be back."

"Will you ever go back?"

"There was this one time," Sam said, "we were stuck in Kiksadi Bay, waiting out a gale. Even Roy wouldn't risk it, the wind was howling, the seas fifteen feet or more. Nothing to do but drink and sit. Roy was liquored up, you know how his eyes were so deep and black you thought there was no bottom to them? He had us, me and the hunter, in some kind of spell. He told us that everyone was afraid, even him. That what he did was think himself big, the way you do when a bear is bluffing you. You know how a bear turns to the side when it sees you, shows you the biggest part of its body? You do that, he said. Take out all the tools, he said, your courage, your hammer, your ax. Bluff this country right back, and sooner or later you won't be afraid anymore. What shit have they been feeding you all your life, he said. You can do anything, he said, don't let anyone tell you different. How could I go back home, Winnie?"

Sam seemed to shake himself out of the memory with physical effort, picking up his canteen and taking another long drink. "She didn't walk the coast," he said. "Do you still want to turn back?"

I regarded what lay ahead of us. Looking carefully, I could see the places where someone slim and unsubstantial could weave through the branches like a ghost, leaving no trace of her presence. That hope allowed me to pull myself to my feet. Birdman hooted far ahead of us, and we hollered back.

"So we go on," Sam said. He shoved the canteen back in his pack. "I'll be right beside you. You can count on that."

But he was wrong. Soon we were forced apart by the trees. I lost him in the dark woods and did not see him again for hours.

Eleven

I arrived at the red cliffs at the moment when the sun decided to slip below the horizon. Darkness spilled over the rock face and into the clearing. The eyes of little animals traced fiery patterns through the dusk as they scattered for shelter.

The others came from the forest after me one by one, looking as if they had been in a fierce clash with the woods. We stood taking inventory of each other. Already everyone bore battle scars: Birdman limped more than usual, and a lump slowly rose on Sam's forehead where a stout branch had kicked back against his face. My legs were scraped, my hair a tangled mass down my back.

"We made it," Sam said, dropping his pack and windmilling his arms. I knew what he was thinking. Nobody would go through the cedar forest on purpose. Nobody except the hopeless or the very determined.

We set up camp in the muskeg, unwilling to go on at night into an unexplored country. Though we carried headlamps, it would be easy to bypass something important, a clue. A small footprint pressed into the mud. A scrap of clothing, caught by the arms of a passing bush. Even the easiest way to pass through the landscape. Instead we settled in for the night, building a small fire and tying the ends of a tarp to the trees.

Huddled up next to a small slice of muskeg, the cliffs glowed with a strange light. This was ultramafic rock, Birdman told us, placing his hand on a slab. Volcanic intrusions, brimming with iron that stained the rock red. This type of rock was as substantial as we could hope for. Our feet would stick to it even at a dangerous angle, but in places the weather was slowly crumbling the rock into tiny pebbles. We would have to be careful. We would have to respect the rock.

"We live in a ring of fire," he explained, drawing a map in the ashes of our own fire. The map circled up toward Redoubt in the north, the most famous volcano of all, and down through the archipelago toward the lights of Seattle. It was a wide, sprawling circle of earthquakes and volcanoes, the tectonic plates moving uneasily beneath the surface. North of here, flaky ash from an eruption hundreds of years ago made up one layer of the soil, a lighter-colored band in a dark cake.

This was a dynamic land, he went on, the strange light from the cliffs falling on his face. It shifted always under the pressures of rock and sea. Years ago an earthquake had caused a massive landslide, a whole section of cliff buckling into the water. He had seen the scar of the resulting wave, seventeen hundred feet up a mountain, scraped bald and treeless.

This was the most I had heard Birdman say at one time, and the effort seemed to drain him. He hunched down on his heels to stir a pot of rice and beans and said no more for a while.

Sam and I sat by the fire. It was the closest I had ever been to him besides the time in the pantry when I thought that I could feel the heat from his body radiating out toward me. Probably it was just the fire, a trick of the cliffs and the wind conspiring together, but I found that I was warm for the first time since I had come back to Never Summer Bay.

"Why did you go, Winnie?" Sam asked. "I woke up that day and you were gone."

Sam's room above the boathouse had been barely big enough to fit him. It was an afterthought, cobbled together with scraps of plywood and reached by an uncertain set of wobbly stairs. The only sounds he could hear from his one window were the slap of water on the dock and the gentle nudges of boats against buoys. Down at the boathouse, you could pretend not to know anything. Instead you could whistle your way through each night, concerned only with the way the wind howled through the bay, the old trees straining with each blow. The only way to know what was happening up at the lodge was for someone to tell.

I searched for words. It wasn't just the two of them and their unending dance that I had tried to escape. I realized now that I had needed to leave to decide what kind of woman I would be. Would I be like the bear hunters' wives, forever one step behind their husbands, burdened with the responsibility of staying beautiful, or would I become a woman who let a man carve his way into her body and mind? I wanted to be neither, but I had no others to choose from in Never Summer Bay.

"My father was a dangerous man," I told him finally. "Surely you knew that."

"Roy taught me everything about this coast," Sam said. "I can still see him, floppy salt-stained hat on his head, showing me how to tie a bowline. Took me forever to get it right, but he wouldn't give up on me. If you can't tie knots, tie a lot, he used to say. He saw something in me that nobody else ever had. I liked it, that he believed in me. I knew he wasn't even keel, but I didn't want to know what else might be going on at night after I closed my door."

"Nobody wanted to know."

"There was one time," Sam said. "Someone hadn't tied a boat up tight enough, and it was driving me crazy, banging against the dock. I knew I would get chewed out for it in the morning, so I went out to fix it. Althea was out there with an ice pack from the freezer.

She had built a little fire on the beach and was tending it. Her eyes were bright as stars. I don't know where you were that night. An accident, she said, fell down the stairs. I knew she wasn't telling the truth, but she made me promise not to do anything. Promise me, she kept saying. It will be all right, it always is, she said."

He sighed. "I've often asked myself one question," he said. "Why did I let myself get so tangled up in your family? And I keep coming back to that first day. You three belonged here, just like the salmon and the bears. It's what I've been looking for, seems like forever. Being here was like learning a whole new language, one you three already knew."

He watched me rebraid my hair, the long strands slipping out of my fingers before I could capture them. "I probably shouldn't tell you this, but even though I could sense something wasn't right over there in the lodge, I thought if I told anyone then it all would change for me. I'd be out of a job, back on the street again. Back on that same damn bar stool that they were saving for me. Heading back home to people who told me I would be back within a month because I didn't have what it took to make it up here."

I was silent. To me, how we lived was how everyone lived. The clients brought their own stories of trees that changed color and buildings that shut out the sky, but those things never seemed real to me. "You're so lucky to get to live here," they would say sometimes, strapping their Rolexes and worried expressions back on as the plane came in to bring them back to their lives. Even though they said it, I sensed that they would not want to stay, that they were ready to leave us behind.

"You have to understand, to me this place is pure magic. Roy was magic. I didn't want it ever to end."

I understood. I remembered the afternoons where it felt like I had been dreaming awake, following my mother down the beach under a rain so light it was like something else, rain and not quite.

"When the hunts were done for the season and I'd be down guiding in Panama, I'd lie on that boat sweating and dreaming of the coast," Sam went on. "Each year I both couldn't wait to come back and was afraid to come back, but in the end this place always won out."

"Why did you keep coming back if you were afraid?"

Now the rain had crept up on us without us noticing. It scrabbled on the tarp like tiny claws. Birdman dished up a plate and retreated far beneath the tarp, chewing in silence. His eyes were half closed, but I knew he missed nothing.

"It's like this," Sam said. He had not touched his food. "There were minutes, hours even, when everything just clicked into place. The boat would be humming along, no rocks in sight, no kelp to foul the prop, water pancake flat. Roy let me take the wheel and he took a nap on the bow, trusting me. Those minutes would add up into days, I thought, until it could last for the whole season. Then the next day the fog would come in, a whole night of it, we'd run aground because I screwed up with the depth finder, and things would go to hell. That's the way it always was. Hell and heaven all in one day."

Something he said sparked a memory. *The night of the fog.* I had forgotten it up until now, but I suddenly remembered the piece of paper, hidden in the pocket of my jacket. It wasn't my mother's handwriting, or my father's either. Who had written it and what did it mean?

Hundreds of clients had passed through the lodge, hundreds of people with their own tragedies and dreams. Pillows got moved around all the time; each spring we had aired them out during a hint of sun to keep the mold at bay. It was entirely possible that some lonely wife had carried a love letter with her to Alaska and hidden it there at some point, pushed it deep into the feathers where it would never be found. Or maybe some of the couples that came together on bear hunts were entwined more than their respective spouses knew. There were all sorts of secrets in the world.

I thought of the secret that Sam carried.

"Tell me what happened to him. With the bear. How did it happen?"

The silence between us went on for so long that I thought he wasn't going to speak. I thought that I could hear my own heart beating over the lazy flap of the tarp. How could Sam not hear it? How was I still sitting here anchored to the earth, just a sliver of darkness separating the two of us? Enchantment Bay was a place that I had held in my heart for years. Each time my father had raised his voice, I let myself slip back to that time. It was the best memory I had of my father.

Finally Sam said, "We were between clients. Just the three of us in the lodge. Ernie came by one night with the barge. He stopped in for a beer. We talked a little about what he had seen going on up and down the coast, you know, like he does. This time he told us that the word in town was that there was going to be a timber sale in Enchantment Bay. The cruisers were in there, marking the trees with blue paint. Life and death, they got to choose."

I could imagine my father sitting at the table, simmering with a stew of frustration and rage. I could see him pacing, his body seized with the need to do something, anything.

"So Roy, he thought he should go there to see what was happening. He never hunted the alder tunnels. He left those bears alone. He respected them. They were the oldest, smartest bears, he used to say. Bears that were so smart they turned nocturnal so that they could have nothing to do with us. We have to do something, he said. The bears need us to do something.

"What can we do, I asked him. I knew we couldn't fight it. Just let it go, I said. It's only one bay. There's plenty of others. The bears will adapt. They'll move."

He sighed. "You know, he yelled at me a lot. Yelled when I wasn't quick enough with the net. Yelled when I spooked a bear. I was used to it, the yelling. He always calmed down eventually, it blew over, he acted like it never happened. He didn't yell this time though. He just looked real sad and said, 'What happens to those trees happens to all of us.'"

He would think that, I knew. Sometimes late at night, when there was nothing but rain and darkness, my father would hold forth to his captive audience. Bear and salmon, salmon and trees, he lectured. A circle of life and death. Take too many of one out of the equation and the circle is broken. We have to be careful, become architects of this world we are given, he would say. Listening, I had been unsure. This country seemed so big, sprawling out like an outstretched hand. How could we make a dent in it? But then I would see the bear skins draped over the boat and know that it was possible.

"Roy told me and Ernie that things were changing, faster than we could even measure. Thunderstorms, when we'd never even seen lightning here in Southeast before. The glacier on Mount Snowy, getting smaller every year. Now the trees. A man can either shove his head in the sand or make a stand, he said to us. You know what kind of man I am, he told us."

Sam picked up a boot and studied it. "Nothing ever dries out here," he said. He did not meet my gaze. "There were a pair of timber cruisers in the bay, kids. From what Roy told me after, a bear had been in the area. They got spooked and shot. Not a kill shot. You know what happens with that."

Suddenly cold, I shuffled closer to the fire. "You can't leave a wounded bear out there. It lies in wait for you. Is that what happened? Did he stumble onto the bear without knowing?"

Sam said, "He told me to stay back at the lodge. I think he knew there would be trouble. But after he left, Althea asked me to follow him in the skiff. She made me promise. I remember it was the most beautiful day. The way the sun danced on the waves."

It seemed to me that Sam paused a little too long. Then he said, "I decided to wait for Roy at the boat. I didn't know about the bear yet. I had to stay with the boat. Tide was falling. You know how quick it falls in that shallow bay."

I nodded. Even with a good Indian anchor, things sometimes went wrong. Then someone had to swim for it or wait for the tide to turn. It was possible.

"But you were always with him, though," I said.

Sam looked away. "Not that time. Not when it counted."

The wood was wet and smoke stung my eyes. I drew a deep breath.

"What happened after that?"

"He was in the hospital for a while. There were surgeries. He had to learn to walk again, as much as he can walk. Work the chair. See through one eye. Finally they let him out, had to, no health insurance in the bear hunting business. But things changed after that. Business dropped off. Way off. News got around. Bookings were cancelled. The booking guy in Anchorage quit. Nobody wanted to go hunting with him, people said he was unsafe. I told you he kind of operated on a shoestring anyway. Now it got worse. The other guides talked it up; they loved it. Less competition for them. They never liked him anyway; he never shared information with them, never helped anyone out. Roy couldn't pay me anymore, but I stuck around. Just for a year, I thought. Just to make sure they would be okay."

I should have come sooner. I did not realize I had whispered those words aloud. They were almost lost in the crackle of the fire, but Sam heard. He leaned in so close that our foreheads almost touched. I was surrounded by the scent of him. There was the acrid tang of his wool coat, washed a million times but saturated forever with the reek of fish, the clean scent of freshly cut spruce, wood smoke that coated his hair.

I swam in his scent like a salmon up a river, closing my eyes.

"Winnie," Sam said. "Look at me." He tipped up my chin with two fingers and looked right at me so intently that it felt like he could see all the way down inside to where everything simmered: fear, regret, sorrow.

"You did nothing wrong," he said. "Believe me?"

I whispered, "Did they ever talk about me?"

"Fire's dying," Sam said. He dropped his hand. "It's not worth the fight to keep it alive, is it? You know that they kept things on the surface with me. Once Roy told me that I had to quit asking about you. You would come back when you had found whatever it was you were looking for. I think they were just letting you go, Winnie. Isn't that what you wanted?"

I had wanted more than that. I wanted some kind of magic, like the kind in my mother's stories, the kind where good always triumphed over evil in the end, a hero realizing the error of his ways, the poison draining out, the curse lifted. I wanted them to grow entwined like trees, not two people on either side of a ragged, angry line. I had wanted the impossible.

Sam gave up on his boots and pulled them on, wincing as the water sloshing inside met his feet. "It just about killed us to see him out there on the dock, day after day. He kept trying to walk more than a few steps without the cane, without the chair. He was determined to get back to the way he was, no matter what the doctors had told him. He kept falling, clawing his way back up, over and over, until we got damn sick of it, but what could we do? He never would listen, wouldn't accept our help. Not a damn cripple, he would snap. Then one day he just stopped. He had enough of the fight, I guess."

The fire sizzled with each drop of rain that reached it. Fires here provided more smoke than heat, the heartwood steeped in water that had fallen as rain or percolated in from fog. Here water and wood were not two separate things, but one single entity, impossible to separate.

"Waiting," Sam went on, even though I had not spoken. "Waiting for bookings that never came. And every day seeing the helicopters bring cruisers in, bay by bay. It broke his heart."

I bowed my head, an invisible weight settling on my shoulders. The timber sales must have been a conquering flag run up a pole, a reminder of the real world that my father had tried to shut out with his barricades and guns and bad temper. I had always sensed the danger of the rest of the world, hovering out there somewhere past the points of our bay, past the mountains, past everything I knew and could see. Now it was here.

"They are all going to be clear cut, all these bays, starting next summer. Trees cut, sent to Japan."

A light scatter of rain pitted the tarp. Long skirts of cloud brushed the mountains, shutting out the way we had come and the miles we still had to go. It felt lonesome here, cupped in the palm of this valley, as if we were the only three people left in the world.

The timber sales, the accident, my mother's disappearance: it was all adding up to the one moment that my father had made a decision that he could not reverse. The ladder had disintegrated into a few rotten boards, not enough for someone to pull themselves out of the grip of the ocean. Even someone who changed his mind and tried. Especially not someone with beach stones in his pockets and an even heavier weight in his heart.

The tarp lifted under the moan of the wind. Now rain hit it like gunshots.

The memory of my mother's letter burned inside me. What my father had asked her to do I could not keep to myself. "I thought it might have been just one of her stories. You know how she liked to tell stories. I thought she might be trying to get me to come back. I thought maybe he wasn't as desperate as she made it sound."

"I figured that was what he was after," Sam said. "Roy Hudson wasn't a man who gave up easily. When the fight went out of him, he was as good as gone already."

"Did he ever ask you the same thing he asked her?"

"No. He wouldn't have. I wasn't someone he would have turned to for that. I knew something was passing between them, but to be honest, I didn't want to be part of it."

He guessed the question I did not want to ask.

"And I couldn't have done it, either, even though it tore me up to see him that way. It's a fact, I thought sometimes it would be better if he was to stop breathing in the night, but no, I would never have helped him do it. Would you have done the same?"

My father on the beach last night, caught hard between a whiskey bottle and the sea. The silhouette of his chair on the dock, a chair he would always need. Never again to feel the wind in his hair as he piloted a boat in clean carving turns through the ocean, dodging driftwood and rocks. Never again to be the star of the show.

The fire sang with each leap of the flames. "No," I said finally. I pictured myself with cold aluminum under my fingers. The ocean, waiting. My mind shrank back from the final push. "Nothing he said could have made me come close."

I had always thought of my father as the bravest man alive. He threw himself into life without reservation. "I've got this," he would say when facing a sea white with foam or a sulky client who couldn't shoot straight. There was no room for doubt in my father's mind. Despite all this, it had taken him months to summon up the courage to end his life. Only now could I see that his bravery might have been a mask covering up secret fear.

"We understand each other, then," Sam said. "I thought we might. None of you really knew me back then, or wanted to know me. I had a purpose just like the boats did. Just like the guns did. Am I right?"

A protest died on my lips. Though I had dreamed about Sam most nights, the Sam I had created in my head was someone braver and stronger. He had been someone without a fault line, someone who would take me away from my hiding place. An escape route. The Sam I saw now was nothing like that imaginary man.

But still. There had been that moment when he looked at me as if he knew everything about me that there was to know.

"Now that Roy's gone, after this, after we find her, I thought I might like a little cabin somewhere. Maybe there's something dirt cheap for sale with a river because that makes for the best sleeping. Maybe it would be in the Rocky Mountains. Montana. Idaho. Kick around the Rock Creek country where it's not so damn wet all the time."

Sam fiddled with the fire, pushing the embers closer together with a stick. "You should see it there, Winnie. In the fall the leaves on the trees turn yellow as your hair. When the wind blows it's the prettiest sight you've ever seen."

Without looking at me, speaking so softly I had to lean close to hear, he said, "Thought maybe you might want to go there with me."

Had he really said those words or had I imagined it? But there he was, looking intently at me, waiting for me to answer.

I stared down at my boots, suddenly shy.

It had always seemed to me that nothing or no one person would ever stick to Sam. My father had teased him about the bear hunters' wives. Many of them had hung onto Sam's arm just a little too long when being helped from the boat, had casually wandered down to the dock, cocktail in hand, to "help" him with a chore. They sauntered down to the boathouse and threw pebbles at his window, giggling. "Sam!" they called in city voices. "Come out and play!"

He treated them all the same though, with a studied indifference, escaping from them as soon as he could, one light in his room burning half the night. "Sam, he's afraid of women," my father had hooted, raising a glass in a toast. He then lowered his voice. "Maybe he plays for another team." The wives tittered, clinking their glasses to his. Each one, I had thought, secretly believed she would be the one to make him crack. Failing that, they turned to my father, a much more receptive source.

"Why me?" I asked now, thinking of all of those possible women. "Why not someone else?"

"Winnie," Sam said. His voice was still low; I had to strain to hear. "Don't you know by now? I was waiting for you to really see me."

I froze. It seemed to me as if everything paused too. Even the wind that had been worrying the tips of the bushes stilled to a whisper. The rain that had been dripping over the side of the tarp suddenly stopped. The whole world seemed to wait.

"Listen," Sam said, "you're different than all of the others. You're not hard yet. Know what I mean?"

He saw that I didn't. "Other women, they've got this hard shell over them. It's like that candle wax on the lodge table, remember how it built up? Took a hell of a job to chip it off? Those women, you can't chip away at them to see who they really are. They've hardened over, a guy doesn't have a chance. You're not like that yet."

I remembered the candles flickering in the dark night, my father sitting up late with the bear hunters' wives, the men passed out long before, my mother a silent storm cloud upstairs. The voices, low, teasing, too low for me to understand. His unsteady steps on the stairs, finally, late, too late for normal people. The wives' foot-falls, reluctant and slow, down to where their forgotten husbands snored.

"Always wondered what went on in the big house at night," Sam said. "All those candles, it took hours for them to burn down. What were you all doing up there?"

Sam threw the stick in the fire and it blazed up briefly. We both watched it crumble into ash. I thought of what story my mother and I could make up about this. *What if you have loved someone since you were fifteen? What if just being near him makes fog roll around in your head? What do you do then?*

Before I could answer, he said, "Listen to me. The wilderness must be making me crazy. Forget what I said, all right?"

Without looking at me, he got up and went over to where his sleeping bag was laid out. Come back, I wanted to say, but I didn't. The seconds ticked by and the moment was lost.

I sat next to the fire, its heat not enough to warm me. My body felt too small to contain the heart within. It felt swollen past its normal size, bouncing around in there with nothing to contain it. I thought that this might have been what my mother felt in the Hell and Gone, cigarette smoke over the day-drinking fishermen and over her like a second skin, the smell of sweat, fish, and desperation a bubbling stew she could almost taste. I could see it as if I had been there that day. My father striding in with his mind on a pint, slapping hands with the bar line-up.

The bartender would have rung the brass bell: my father, buying the house a round. Cheers going up and down the bar. She lifted her head to see a sparkplug of a man, only a head higher than herself, the rain dripping off his dark hair and beard, his black eyes snapping with life. He moved through the dust and lost dreams of the bar with a kind of grace that she only imagined could exist. He reached for her hand.

Standing there, she felt as though she had swallowed the sun.

Birdman crept out to join me with a flask and a rifle, pulling his hood over his face against the rain. Grateful for his silence, I reached deep in my pockets for warmth. The paper I had hidden there was sodden now. Of course, not a client's wife, I realized. A client's wife would have long ago destroyed this secret souvenir or taken it with her. Someone had written this to my mother.

I ran through a list in my head. Not Ernie; he often brought his Russian mail-order wife along with him on his trips. Equally stout, apple-cheeked, and indistinguishable in their Helly Hansens, they were inseparable. There were the clients, but they blew through in ten-day spans, and if they left gifts, they were mostly for my father;

my mother and I just servants acknowledged only for the hearty meals we provided before each trip. We blended into the paneling, merely women who could not possibly understand the thrill of hunting. Women who did not look like the wives with their useless suede boots and tightly curled hair. Women who did not resemble the platinum blondes with naked skin as smooth as paint in the men's magazines they snuck onboard the boat.

There had been assistant guides, several of them, lasting only for short spans. There had been fierce arguments out by the dock, each guide storming off onto a floatplane announcing that he would return only when hell froze over and he would make sure that any prospective applicants in town knew not to come either. My mother and I watched this from the sidelines, knowing not to grow accustomed to any of the men who came and went with the regularity of the seasons.

Who else had there been? Our world was so small.

There was only one other person it could have been.

Althea, Roy, and Dean. They both were in love with her, but she chose Roy.

I drew in my breath.

"What is it?" Birdman asked, already taking the rifle off his shoulder.

Dean. It had to be. Who else could it be?

I looked at Birdman's concerned face, a moon above his dark clothes.

He flew like he didn't care if he made it back. My uncle had been in love with my mother. Had she loved him back? Had my father known?

All along I believed that my mother and I had no secrets. We shared everything—clothes and the halves of our sandwiches and the things that made us happy: a spray of blueberries, the fresh wash of sunlight through clouds. Even the things that made us afraid, like the deep rip current that lurked near the Trader Islands, forcing us to back paddle in our kayaks. The black-and-white slice of orcas through the water. The threat of a tsunami, born of an earthquake far out to sea, rolling in without warning. Now I realized that I had known only what was on the surface, the things easily seen.

I handed Birdman the note, explaining where I had found it and who I thought it was from. He clicked on his headlamp and squinted at it, his glasses covered in steam. "What does this mean? The night of the fog," he said. "Why would she keep this? One night they were together? A night she regretted ever since? Or a night she never forgot?"

"Maybe both." It was impossible to know. There were many foggy nights, nights in which we were muffled in white as thick as wool, nights when I had not even been able to see where land ended and sea began. Fog made my mother a little crazy, more reckless than I had ever seen her. "I want to scream," she would say. "Run barefoot through the woods. Swim across the ocean." In the end she did neither of those, just barricaded us into the lodge as if the fog could steal in through the doors and suffocate us.

Often this would happen when the men were out on a hunt, and there had been times when Dean had flown in to the lodge and was trapped there, waiting for their return. Anything could have happened on those nights, because they shut me out with their adult talk and glasses of wine. Bored, I would wander upstairs to my radio and the voices of people I would never know. The lights downstairs burned late on those nights.

On those nights the clients missed their flights back to the Lower 48 because even my father wouldn't risk taking his boat from a sheltered bay out onto the ocean and back to the lodge. His radar was spotty and the rocks uncharted. Better to stay in place and wait it out. The fog put everyone on edge, but everyone also knew that it was better to hunker down in the bay you knew than to risk it on the ocean. It was sometimes days before anyone could move.

"I never saw anything," I said. But I knew something had happened. I could feel it, like the last piece of a jigsaw puzzle pressed into place. This would explain the way my mother stared at the map. The way she seemed to sometimes deliberately place herself near my father when he was in one of his stormy moods. Had it been guilt, sadness, regret?

"Something could have gone on between the two of them," Birdman said. "Maybe she wanted the easy way for a change. The sweet without the bitter. Doesn't take much to make a mistake. Too much red wine, too much fog, what's the difference, you think. World still turns. Tide still goes out. If I knew Roy, he spread himself thin over there in Never Summer, between the hunters and the weather and the work. Didn't leave a lot of time for her in the mix."

"The bear hunters' wives," I said, remembering again the shadows of candles on the walls. "They used to drape over him like sweaters. We used to laugh at them in the kitchen, but I think she hated the way he used to dress for dinner when the boat was in, to impress them. Cuff links, ironing his one white shirt, apricot pomade in his hair. They came in the kitchen wanting more wine and told her how lucky she was to have a man like him. She didn't like sharing him with them. She was glad when the plane left."

"Dean took it hard, her not choosing him," Birdman said thoughtfully, stroking his beard. "The day she went off with Roy, he went down the coast and didn't come back for a long time. Probably he never gave up trying, all those years after. He wasn't a man who would ever give up trying as long as he could see a sliver of hope to weasel through. Kind of the same way he flew."

I hung over Birdman's shoulder, seeing what had only briefly registered before. The note was torn from a pilot's log, the kind that was used to record flight times and fuel consumption. I had seen this same type of logbook many times in Uncle Dean's plane, spattered with the ancient remains of coffee and curling up from humidity. He had shoved a pencil behind his ear, brow furrowing as he attempted to do the math. In the end he usually shrugged and scribbled down any numbers he dreamed up. "Screw the FAA," he said, and chuckled. "What are they going to do, ground me for not adding right?" He always flew like that, trusting in what he saw out of his window more than his instruments to keep him safe.

Dean's logbook. His hand with the finger torn off by the prop, writing a note to someone who, in the end, did not choose him. Flying into the teeth of a storm because he did not care if he ever made it back.

Birdman clicked off his headlamp and handed me the paper. I held on to it for a minute before I placed it on the fire. For a thing with so much weight and history, it blazed up fast and was gone in seconds. "Well," he said. "So that's that."

"I never really knew her," I said. It came out all wrong, almost a sob.

I could tell Birdman did not know what to say, but he let me rest my head on the scratchy cloth of his jacket. If his muscles tensed up because of how close we were, I could barely feel it.

I thought that maybe he was thinking of his own daughter, somewhere out there in the world growing up. What would she know about him when she was older? It would not be the Birdman I knew, quiet and kind, but someone else, someone distant and unforgiving, someone who could track any animal but could not find her. There were so many different ways to see people.

"I'm not one to judge, if that's what she did. We shone being around those boys," Birdman said. "Me, Isaiah, her, we all shone so bright. Couldn't last, nothing that burns that hot ever does. But I'll tell you what, it's good while it lasts."

He dropped a log on the fire. "They weren't solid, those boys, not the way Sam is. When I look at a tree, I can see how sound the wood is, if there's heart rot or fungus or something else eating away at it inside. Sam's as sound as they come. Not a lot of fire, but he'll last."

I remembered what Sam had told me in the cedars, and I imagined him leaving me one day, in search of someone new. "I don't know if he can stick," I said.

"Some people don't know when to let go, either," Birdman said, and I wasn't sure if he meant my father or my mother, or maybe both.

The world seemed to me to be such an uncertain place. One wrong step and there you were, knee deep in trouble. Each word seemed so irrevocable, unable to take back. Making choices seemed too dangerous.

I thought that instead I could sit here until the moss covered me up and I belonged to this mountain. Let the rain pour holes into my heart, sink deeper into the muskeg until roots bound me to this place.

I leaned forward and plucked a shooting star, twirling it in my fingers. This had always been my favorite flower. It was one of the early ones, bravely poking its head out into the snow before the other flowers dared. It stayed late too, as if it didn't want to miss a thing. Its purple petals were spread like a dancer's skirt, the whole flower dart shaped, poised for flight. This flower didn't seem afraid of anything, even though its heavy head bobbed on a stalk that seemed too tender and thin.

"How do you ever know what's right?" I asked, but Birdman only shrugged. He had no answer to that, he told me. Nobody did.

"You just go until you get cliffed out, or until the mountains bite back. Then you backtrack and pick a different route. Roy's told you which way to go all your life, but now it's up to you to choose."

It didn't seem fair to me. I wanted a map like the salmon had. I wanted to swim out to sea the way they did, until a signal told them two years later that it was time. The same thing happened to whales as they slowly swam between Hawaii and this coast. It sometimes seemed like everyone and everything knew where to go except me.

"The last time I saw Angela, she was six," Birdman said. He produced a pipe from his pocket and puffed thoughtfully. "This was years ago, when I was a different person. Her mother, my wife once, was hustling her away from me into an Impala and she was crying. Daddy, she screamed. *I want my Daddy*. My wife didn't listen. *He's a no-good, lazy son of a bitch*, I heard her say as they got in the car. *Would rather sit in the woods than get a job like a real man*. I still re-member Angela's face in that dirty window. I never saw her again."

How did he stand it? How did anyone stand all the things that happened in their whole life? Each thing seemed to add up until the load of them was too much to bear. It was enough to make you roll down a dock without a brake. Enough to walk into the woods and never come back.

"Look, though," Birdman said. His gesture took in the glow from the cliffs and the dark pooled water on the muskeg. It included the watchful trees, slowly turning the clearing into a forest. It meant everything, the rain, the unseen mountains above us, and the little creatures we could hear busily burrowing through their night errands.

"There's always some reason to get up in the morning," he said. "Sometimes you have to hunt hard for it, but it's there."

"My father," I began. Birdman nodded. "Sometimes people get tired of hunting," he said.

"Couldn't you go find Angela?" I asked. "Tell her it wasn't like she thought? That you never meant to abandon her?"

Birdman thought for a minute. "The world is so big," he said. I wanted to argue. There were telephone books; I had seen them in town. He could gather all the ones he could find and look through them until he found Angela's name. He could call her and explain about all the years he had missed.

"Maybe someday, Winnie," he said, but I could tell he had given up on finding Angela, or maybe had lost the courage. Still, I allowed myself a thin ray of hope. Someday Angela might show up in Floathouse Bay, following a tip. Her cinnamon hair would shine brightly against the dull green backdrop as she came in to the dock. She would know his real name, the one he had hidden from us. Birdman would gather her up in a hug that went on forever, and they would never be apart again.

"I like Floathouse Bay," Birdman said. "I like the sameness of it. You wake up, the same tide, going in and out, set your watch by it. The deer on the beach in winter, whales on their way to Hawaii. No surprises. It's the most peace I've found anywhere."

I knew what he was telling me. He would not be looking for Angela. I had thought of Birdman and Isaiah as sages, honest and true and perfect in ways my father was not, but I realized that they were just men after all. Everyone had their own fault lines. Some were just buried deeper.

I crawled into a borrowed sleeping bag, musky with the scent of all of the other people who had slept in it. It was damp from the surrounding air and did little to warm me. Overhead the tarp covered me, an artificial sky. I imagined that the three of us breathed in unison, each of us with our own fears and hopes and wishes. Was my mother out here? Did she sleep under a tarp like this one, listening to the way it moved with the wind? In my mind, she moved like the bears, keeping to the shadows. We would find her when she wanted to be found.

Twelve

I slowly awoke from a dream of being under the ocean. In the dream, my body was fluid, somewhere between water and flesh, the color of silver. I was a salmon, a whale, or some other creature whose name I did not know. I was looking for something, combing through the kelp forests and the offshore reefs, around all the islands that were really mountains bursting out of the sea's floor. It was a map I was hunting. A way home.

I was tangled in the sleeping bag, my heart pounding. The tarp sagged above my face, casting a blue light over everything. I was not in the ocean. I was in a muskeg with two men I hardly knew. My father was dead. My mother, gone somewhere in the wilderness.

Sam was crouched on his heels stirring a pot of oatmeal. His hood was pushed back and a fringe of hair fell over his collar. He whistled. A light rain pitted the tarp and a breeze fanned it slightly, sending a fine mist over my face. Sometime in the night rainfall had collected in the center of the tarp, the edges not pulled tightly enough, and now water poured over the sides, spattering everyone inside. A muskeg was not a perfect place to camp either; the downside of sleeping in the open meadow was a slow seeping of water into anything that lay on the ground. I could feel it under the sleeping pad, a river moving underneath.

"Today we climb the cliffs," he said, catching my movement. There was fear in his voice, fear that matched my own. Only Birdman seemed immune to it, his hands shoved in jacket pockets. After lying under the bodies of dead soldiers, listening for the welcoming sound of a helicopter, I imagined that it would take more than the cliffs to scare him. He was in his element out here, moving through the landscape in a graceful way that he did not possess inside of walls.

We ate oatmeal in silence. My thoughts churned through the same groove from the day before. Was this the story my mother had been trying to tell me with each tale she made up? My mother and Uncle Dean involved in a secret love affair. Even if she had known there were so many ways to fall from the sky, even if she knew that after so many years, nobody could survive in this wilderness. Years passed but she never forgot. She had to see. After all, you could fly into a box canyon in the fog and slam into an unseen mountain. You could tumble end over end, punched down by the wind like a giant's fist. You could scrape the edges of the tall trees, flying too close to what pilots called the deck—the solid line of land or sea. Or your plane could just quit flying, but over a spiky peak somewhere, no chance to save it. Better to think of Dean living it up at a lake by his own choosing than any of those other ways. In the end, had she chosen to believe what could not possibly be true?

Why had she left my father now, when he had needed her the most? Surely there had been a better time to climb to the Lake of the Fallen Moon. When clients still clomped up and down the stairs, chunks of mud falling off their boots, their chubby city faces flushed with excitement and fear. When the house was still, the hunt on, bays and bays away from here, time heavy on her hands. There were plenty of times she could have left. Maybe she really had fallen or slipped or been surprised by a bear.

Sam came back from a pothole, the stack of rinsed bowls in his hands. He set them down with a clatter. "Remember what Roy used to say? If it weren't for the rain this would be just like California," he said. "There would be roads all over this valley, houses on those cliffs. The rivers would be dammed and all the bears shot out, he said. Roy was wrong, though. People need sunshine." He placed the bowls in his pack. "This is no way to live. When this is over, I'm heading to the desert. A place so hot you burn your feet crossing it. Where you wear sunglasses all day and night. Where you have to sit under a shade tree to stay cool. What do you think, Winnie?"

"I might want to stay here," I said. My voice sounded small. "In Never Summer."

As soon as I said it, it sounded right. I tested it again. "I'd live in the lodge. Maybe show people the bears. Not to kill them, but to learn about them."

"Isn't this the place you wanted to leave?" Sam said, but he was wrong. It hadn't been the place at all. Without my father, possibly without my mother, it was just another bay. There was nothing re-markable or terrifying about it. Nothing that I needed to escape.

Birdman appeared by my shoulder, startling me the way he always did with his ability to move undetected.

He opened one hand.

"I found this last night when I had to get up to water a tree. I was shining my headlamp around a bit and saw it hanging off that bush over there. Right over there where the cliffs meet the muskeg."

A pale blue ribbon fluttered in his hand. I snatched it from him, but as I took it, the fragile band crumbled into tiny pieces. I watched as they tumbled from my grasp and into the fire where they shriveled and burned in a flash of heat and light.

"Is it hers, Winnie?" Sam asked. "Can you tell?"

I stared into the fire, uncertain. My mother had given up on ribbons long ago. Useless pretty things without a purpose, she told me. Like painting your nails to a glossy sheen, or swiping color across your face. What good did those things do out here, where your feet were covered in rubber boots all of the time and your face wet from rain? But there had been times when she wavered, especially when the bear hunters' wives wafted down to dinner in a cloud of perfume. On those days she had stood in front of the mirror, carefully lining her eyes with gold.

Nobody else ever walked through the cedars without us knowing, unless they had come the long way, across the island. Had it been someone else entirely, marking his safe return from a long trip? The scientists, somehow circumventing our bay and circling back on top of the divide? Was this ribbon left over from Search and Rescue's ground search? Or was it from my mother, marking a path for us to follow?

"I don't know," I said. "It could be."

I closed my eyes, trying to summon her. I sent something with wings out into the forest. *Where are you? Is this a sign?* I felt nothing in return.

We had seen nothing else, although Birdman reminded us that there were a thousand ways to move through the cedars. Only luck would have allowed us to stumble upon the path she had taken. There could be a hundred ribbons in the cedars, and we would never have seen them. At the same time, the part of me that still believed in stories and magic saw my mother placing it here for me to find.

"If it's hers, there's only one way she could have gone from here," Birdman said. He was right. The cedars hugged the cliffs tight around our slice of muskeg. You would need wings unless you chose to climb.

I felt a fierce surge of possibility that even the rain could not dim. We kicked over the ashes of the fire and shook out the tarp, each of us taking one corner and walking toward each other to fold it up. The only thing that showed we had been here when we were done was the grass, trampled flat beneath our boots. That would recover too, slowly springing up as if we had never passed through.

Over all of us the rain fell. It showed no signs of letting up, just kept falling in a lazy way from the sky, plinking into the small pools and through my hair and down into my boots. It had all the time in the world.

"Bear tracks," Birdman said. They were recent, pooled with the night's rain. As we slept, a sow and cubs had padded past. Muffled by the sound of the tarp, we heard nothing.

"How did they get through the cedars?" Sam asked, but Birdman had no real answers. "Bears can go anywhere, they're like spirits that way." He slid open the rifle's magazine and fit in three fat slugs, clicking them into place. "Running from the boars, the sows do what they have to do sometimes to protect their young," he said.

"I'll carry it today," Sam said. We had all taken turns so far, hoisting the rifle over fallen trees and balancing it on our shoulders where we could.

Birdman handed it over, and Sam slung the rifle over his shoulder. As we cinched on our packs, I thought about the night before and what Sam had told me. Not about the Rocky Mountains—that was too big for me to swallow. When I thought about it, a whole world yawned open, a world far beyond the boundaries I had always known.

I thought instead about his story. Waiting at the boat—something about it didn't ring true. Getting a skiff high and dry was a bad thing, but not something that couldn't be reversed with a little time, strong backs, and tide. You could leave a skiff, especially if you scented trouble in the forest. Worst case, you sat on the beach and waited for the hours to pass and the boat to float again. What had really happened in Enchantment Bay? Did I really want to know? I heard my father's voice. *Don't ask unless you really want to know.*

Maybe it was better to erase the past the way the high tide blotted out the day's stories: dainty deer tracks, the skiff of sand where someone placed a tent, the wash of salty bull kelp. The high tide started a new story, one that would change again at slack. Water was always in a state of restless change. Nothing mattered except for the present.

But I found I wanted to know. Whatever it was, the secret would slowly cut into any sort of future I could have with Sam. It would carve a wedge between us. I would not be able to look at him without wondering what he was keeping from me. There had been enough secrets already.

I watched him as he trudged slowly through the muskeg, scanning the swampy ground for the best route. Muskegs reduced everyone to the same pace. Navigating through them took time and patience. Time to pull each boot firmly out of the mud before it was sucked off our feet. Patience to find the lowest water between drainage channels instead of sloshing through and overtopping boots. Time to toil up one rolling slope and down another, feet sinking deep into the pillowed soil. For all their openness, muskegs yielded no easy passage.

I would find out today, I told myself. Whatever it took, I would know what really happened in the bear tunnels of Enchantment Bay.

Leaving the muskeg, we started up the red cliffs. They loomed over us, keeping us in perpetual shade as we began to climb through a series of ledges. Frost still clung to the small strands of grass that dared to grow in the weaker places. Pieces of rock crumbled through my fingers and my hands were covered with a fine dust as I reached to pull myself higher. We hurried across shelves no wider than our feet, trusting that each step would hold us. Below us the cedar forest receded until it looked harmless and insignificant.

Once we climbed the pockmarked face of the main cliff, the hardest part seemed to be over. A chain of plateaus scissored in front of us toward the divide. This was easy walking, the edges scalloped through erosion but mostly flat as though someone had come along with a giant rolling pin and beat them into submission. We climbed each plateau like we were walking stairs to the sky. Starting with the size of a dinner plate, the plateaus widened until the three of us could walk abreast.

"Are we really doing this?" Sam asked, saying the same thing I was thinking. Each step took us farther away from what we knew, each step irrevocable, making it harder to turn around.

The cliffs moaned and sighed as the wind flowed over them. Gnarled plants clung to crevices, their branches twisted by the ceaseless wind. We sidestepped murky pools draped with lily pads. Strange dark birds flapped silently away from nests. This far above the sea, we were way past tree line, the place where the forest gave up and retreated. There was nowhere to hide up here. These cliffs were fully exposed to the gales that swept across the island, unhindered for sheets of snow and rain, unstopped by terrain or vegetation.

This was a place of firsts. Some plants only grew here, on these cliffs, Birdman told us. This was the only place in the world you could find them. These were the only rocks like this on the coast, forced upward by violence and now weathered by time.

"Hard to find tracks here," he said. We were surrounded by rock, nothing to sink our feet into and leave a print. Turrets of red rock separated us from other paths we could have taken. The plateau we crossed now was fifty feet wide, the bottom slice of a slowly tapering wedding cake.

Sam echoed what I thought we must all be thinking. "This is a hell of a good place to disappear into."

"Let's stay close," Birdman said. "A guy could wander off the edge of this thing and end up a thousand feet below in the ocean without even trying. And look for ribbons as you go."

I was sure there would be more ribbons, a solid line of them pointing the way up the divide. But there was nothing on the cliffs to show that anyone had been there before us. There were only clouds of tiny birds diving for food in the low bushes and the whines of early mosquitoes around our heads. We were walking on faith alone.

Then I saw something that did not belong. Not a ribbon. Not a woman in a brown coat like I thought at first, but a bear, trailed by two pudgy cubs. I had not been paying attention, my eyes focused on the ground we were covering and the cloud of little birds swooping over the low bushes. It was a common error. *Big picture stuff*, my father used to lecture. Take it all in, in one sweeping glance. Don't get caught up in small details. Otherwise it could cost you dearly. Inattention could mean a rock in the prop. Coming hard aground on a sandbar. Anchoring too close to a cliff. Bears where you did not expect to see them, despite this morning's tracks.

The wind was not in our favor, blowing into our faces instead of into hers where she would have smelled us long ago. We were close, too close. Close enough to see the muscles rippling under her skin as she nosed the ground, so close that I could see individual strands of chocolate-colored fur, silver tipped with water. The bear jerked up, startled, and stared deep into my eyes.

I had encountered hundreds of bears before, too many to count. The bears looked me over and moved on, realizing they didn't want to get tangled up in whatever danger I represented. The animals were fat and happy here, my father used to tell me, pacified by a diet of salmon and berries. Not like the barren ground grizzlies of the Interior. Here in Southeast you kept an eye out, always, but nine times out of ten you could say something, anything, and they would move out of the way. It was almost like they rolled their eyes: another human? I waited her out, hoping she would do the same.

"Jesus Murphy, what's a bear doing up here?" Birdman whispered. The cubs scampered closer to their mother, watching for a clue.

The bear stood on hind legs, seeking a better view of the danger. Her front legs pounded back onto the ground and she gave a low growl in warning.

Sam moved quickly as a cat. In seconds he had worked the bolt action, slamming a slug into the chamber. He raised the rifle to his shoulder and looked down the barrel. I saw his trigger finger move.

"No," Birdman shouted, shoving Sam to his knees. The rifle clattered to the ground. With a startled woof, the bear leapt away from us, pounding over the rock plateau and out of sight, her cubs bouncing along behind her.

I dropped down to sit, my body suddenly boneless. Slowly everything returned to normal. A feeble sun poked out from the clouds. The little birds flitted back to the bushes. A mosquito landed on my hand, a little jolt of pain. Looking up, I could see the divide only a few feet above me.

I could hear Birdman, his voice a tight line, keeping emotions in check. "What the hell was that? That bear wasn't going to charge us. What were you thinking?"

Sam rolled over and sat up. He could not meet our eyes. "Hell if I know. For a minute I was back there, in the tunnels," he said. "I could see it happen all over again."

A sharp spike of dread ran through me. Here it was, what I wanted to know. "The bear tunnels? In Enchantment Bay? But you said you weren't anywhere near the tunnels. You were with the boat. Watching the boat. That's what you said! So that it wouldn't go high and dry!"

From somewhere else I watched Birdman put a calming hand on a girl's shoulder. The girl had long hair that strayed from a fat braid. She wore a coat that did not fit her. Her dirty face was streaked with tears.

I imagined that I could feel the red rock pulse beneath me, the heartbeat of the earth pounding through all the layers of heat and stone to reach me. The red cliffs felt solid, something I could lean against while everything else shifted.

I took a long, ragged breath. "I'm not walking another step until I know what happened in the bear tunnels."

Time slowed. Each second stretched out as wide as the sea. I was afraid of what I was about to know. I was afraid that Sam would not say a word. Birdman crouched beside me, his hand the only thing I could count on in the whole world.

Sam rested his chin on his knees. He seemed as unaware of us as the tugboat I could see far out in the strait. The boat steamed along with purpose, pulling a barge. It could be going as far north as Juneau or even farther, Haines or Homer or even Anchorage. For a moment I wished I was on that tugboat, concerned only with quartering the boat into the swell, wondering where to anchor or whether to just roll on through the dark robe of the night until I came to my destination, far away from here.

As Sam spoke I could see it in my head, clear as a movie reel. A man and a woman on a lonely dock, the ripples of a boat wake slowly fading into nothingness. The rumble of a motor receding.

Minutes before they clasped hands across the table, all three of them.

No guns, Althea said.

They locked eyes. No guns, Roy agreed finally.

Now a man and a woman on a lonely dock watch a man they both love at the tiller, curly hair blowing in the wind. He does not look back. He never looks back.

Go after him, she says.

They look at each other.

I don't know, he says. He won't like it.

Please.

He hesitates.

Please.

All right.

Take a rifle with you, she says.

He nods.

Promise me you will keep him safe. Promise me.

Yes. I promise.

He takes the old skiff, because that is all they have left. It needs bailing every few miles; the drain plug is not tight, the gas line troublesome. The daughter, escaping, took the other one. Where was it now? Was she still in Floathouse Bay? Or had she hailed a boat, let the skiff loose with the tide, was it washed up on some beach, a twisted heap of aluminum? Nobody knows for sure, although the last time Ernie came by she was still down coast. That was months ago though, back in the fall. Winter is a season he does not know here. Anything can happen in winter.

He hugs the shore so he won't be seen, keeping an eye on the boat he is following. But the bigger boat is much faster than his aging Lund, and by the time he gets to the bay he is about a half an hour behind. It is anchored, turning lazily with the incoming tide. Nobody is in sight.

It is a bad time to anchor, the tide heading out across the estuary flats in a sweeping curtain. His anchor might not hold. He is still not good at this, even after all these seasons. The boat could drift in, get smashed on the rocks. He waits, thinks about it for a minute. Wouldn't it be better to wait here? He hates himself for his fear, but he always has it. It is a part of him that lurks in the background, a thing he has learned to punch down, but it is always here.

Yes, better to stay here. He will wait, and Roy will come back. Probably it is a false alarm, coast gossip only. They will drive in tandem along the coast, two boats in a parallel line, their wakes crossing each other. He will feel safe, like he always does when Roy is around. Sure, he screws up and Roy yells, but when it comes to finding your way home in a following sea, Roy is the man you want to guide you home.

Then he hears a shot. A scream maybe, it is hard to tell. Impossible to ignore. He shifts from foot to foot. He has to go in.

He leaves the boat with a prayer that the anchor will hold.

He leaves the boat with a prayer he cannot articulate in words.

Because he can do nothing else in this moment, he heads across the flat to the tunnels.

When he gets there, deep in the tunnel, he hesitates, holding the rifle in sweaty palms. He stops far enough away so that he is not seen. Man and bear are so entwined he cannot see where one ends and the other begins. He knows he has to do something, but he is strangely paralyzed. He knows if he moves, gets closer, the bear will see him. It may even drop its victim and come to him. He is not sure he can take an accurate shot from where he is. He could hit the man, not the bear.

The fear washes over him, more powerful than any tide. It is a fear he has carried with him every season, the knot in his stomach when he wakes, the fear that never really goes away. Without thinking he turns and runs, back to the shore, back to safety. The whole way he imagines that he has done this for Roy. That the bear will chase him instead, and he will leap in the boat to safety. Figure it out from there. But he knows that he is lying to himself. The bear was too intent on Roy to even notice Sam was there.

The boat is okay, bobbing slightly in the tide. He cannot go back in there. He is anchored here, for better or worse. He sits slumped on the bow, holding the cold aluminum in blood-drained fingers. What to do. What to do. He hears a shot finally. Not Roy, he didn't have a rifle. The cruisers?

Finally the fog clears in his mind. He goes to the big boat, pulling it to him by the anchor rope. His hands shake. He pulls out the marine radio and calls for help. Even now he can't go back. It's over now, he assumes. He sits there on the boat, waiting for absolution.

"I think Roy saw me," Sam said. "I never asked. He never said a word, after, although there was always this thing between us, something left unsaid. In my dreams I do it right. I go in and shoot the bear. Done it a hundred times for the clients, right? I never missed any of those times. I wouldn't miss this time. Roy gets up and walks out of there. We have a good laugh. Cheated death again, we say. But then I wake up."

I watched one of the birds light on a bush near me. A few wrinkled blueberries clung to its branches. No good now, drained of juice and flavor. Bitter. Even the birds didn't want them.

Sam put his head in his hands, his voice muffled. "The cruiser kid got it together, went in and shot the bear. He had some courage to do that. Courage I didn't have.

"I kept punching this down, but it keeps coming back up until I can't swallow it anymore. The last couple of years I've made up a different ending, where I never go in at all. I thought on it hard enough that after a while I almost started believing it. But just now, with the bears, I was back there in the tunnels. I honestly believed I was there."

I lay flat, pinned by something invisible and heavy on my chest. For the first time I wished to be more like granite than water, my heart encased in thick folds of stone. My eyes ached with the weight of unshed tears. If Sam hadn't run, the bear would not have inflicted so much damage. If the bear hadn't inflicted so much damage, both of my parents would still be living in isolation in Never Summer Bay, the circle unbroken. But was that better than what happened to them in the end?

Sam said, "Believe me, if I could have it to do over I would go the other way. I only got a second to choose and I chose wrong."

I could not force any words to come. They lodged inside of me like bullets frozen in a gun.

"I didn't tell you the truth about Enchantment Bay because after a while I really believed my own story," he said. "I could see the otters rafting up just beyond where I stood in the bay, the mud getting thicker as the tide went out. I could even feel the boat as it bumped against my legs and how I kept pushing it out into deeper water. I know it sounds crazy but that's what I remember when I think about Enchantment Bay. Not the other."

I couldn't look at him. Instead I sat up and looked out over the cliffs. On the ocean side, the cliffs dove abruptly to the water far below. If I looked far out enough I could see the long sweep of Turn Back Strait where it turned to meet the tip of the island and the darker places where rip currents paced through the water. The red cliffs were a strange island in a sea of green and blue.

When the anger came it was like the tide, knocking me off my feet. It was just like the times we had been caught, my mother and me, dreaming out on the flats, not paying attention to the signs. Tide came in a series of inconsequential waves, each stronger than the last, until you were up to your waist, your shoulders, your eyes. Water seemed light until it filled up your mouth and your nose and you were unable to breathe. Anger, it seemed, was the same.

"You were the last person I thought would keep secrets," I screamed. My voice was torn from me and hurled over the cliffs like scraps of paper in a gale. I was screaming as loud as I could and still it was not enough. There was so much country that drowned me out.

Without realizing how it happened, suddenly both of us were standing, my hands curled into fists.

"I thought you were different. I trusted you. Why did you get to choose what truth to tell me? Why did everyone get to choose? When do I get to choose? Tell me! Tell me when I get to be the one to choose!"

My throat was raw, my hair tangled around my shoulders, and tears and rain worked their way down my face. I was hollow all the way down to my bones. The anger left me as quickly as it had come. There had been so much anger, breaking its back over all of us.

I was someone I did not recognize.

"I'm just like him," I whispered.

"You're nothing like him."

I slowly unclenched my fists. "Did I hurt you?"

"You never touched me."

"Oh."

"Winnie," Sam said, "you've never let yourself be angry before. You've pushed it down all your life. This one time doesn't mean you will be like him."

I wanted to believe him.

Birdman was silent, watching us, hunched on his heels. He had started worrying a piece of wood with his knife. The soft heartwood piled up by his feet. "Sort this all out later. Best be moving on," he said. "Not a good place to linger. Go down or go up, those are our choices."

Both men waited for me to choose. I glanced out over the plateau on which we sat. If a plane flew over right now, the pilot would never see us wave. If a boat passenger on the tugboat scanned the cliffs, he would never see us. We did not belong up here. Birdman was right. It was time to go.

For a minute I thought I could go on without either man. I could just follow the hard line of the rocks until I was as high as I could get. Then I would read the country like Birdman was teaching me and find my own way to the lake.

As I thought this I knew that I did not want to go alone. I had come to rely on Birdman's steady presence leading the way and the reassurance of Sam following behind. Bookended between the two, I did not feel so alone.

"Let's keep climbing," I said.

Sam held out a hand. "Truce, for now?"

I considered it. Taking his hand seemed like a betrayal, but even if Sam had stayed in the alder tunnels, would both men have come back alive? There were so many things that could have gone wrong: missed shot, slug caught in the barrel. Misfire. And there was this: How long should he pay for his mistake? He would carry it forever, an unseen anchor tethering him to this coast. No matter where he went, whether it was the desert or the mountains, he would still wake in the night remembering what he had done. Maybe that was enough.

Because I could think of nothing else to do in that moment, because hope was all I had left, I took his hand and took a few shaky steps before I let it go. Without speaking the three of us climbed to the next plateau and then the next, each one skinnier than the last until they ended abruptly near a hanging cirque.

My breath burned in my lungs. This was the highest I had ever been and there was still higher to climb. Looking at Sam, I could tell he was as tired as I was, his head bowed as we paused for a moment in the raw air. With Birdman it was harder to tell. He kept whatever he was thinking deep inside and only pointed to someplace far in the distance.

"That's where the lake sits," he said as the three of us stood together, shivering as the wind burrowed through our clothes. "See the dark rocks above us that look like waves about to break? The lake should be right on the other side."

This was the place, he said, that the glacier had bullied its way through a long time ago, leaving the depression that had slowly filled in with water. This was far above the refugia, that elusive place that the glaciers did not reach, a tiny sliver of land where the bears retreated and began to change. If we had been here thousands of years ago our feet would have been standing on solid ice, the slow rumble of the glacier moving beneath us.

"Winter still in the air," Sam said. It was true. I could feel it in the bite that came off the cliffs. I could see it in the desperate way that the pink monkey flowers reached for the nonexistent sun, growing in profusion, a tiny stream. There was so little time sand-wiched between winters.

A few stubborn trees clung with all their might to the rocks lining the cirque. Elevation and snowpack determined what grew here, and the trees were skirted with denser foliage near their bases where snow lay deep and long. Their ragged bark was punctured with tiny holes, places where wind-driven snow had burrowed in. Only the tough could survive in this transition zone, and the trees were stunted and twisted with effort, the brush a spindly mat.

We were as far from the sheltering forest as we could be. There was a forest in miniature beneath my feet though: a rolling carpet of tiny, red-tipped moss; small, sweet pink flowers; low blueberry shrubs. Clusters of royal blue lupine formed dense mats, their thick fragrance filling the air. My feet sank deep into the tundra, leaving momentary impressions of where I had been.

Ahead was a maze of rough-surfaced rocks. They looked like they had been dropped from the sky, meteors maybe, old stars, I thought. But they were glacial erratics, Birdman told me, rocks dropped there by a slow, lumbering field of ice as it rumbled through thirteen thousand years ago.

"The garden of the giants," Sam said, echoing my thoughts. "Only giants could feel at home here." I could feel him watching me, seeking forgiveness. My thoughts about Sam were all jumbled to-gether like blocks of ice pushed by wind. There was the man I thought I knew and there was also what had been hidden beneath the surface.

Then I forgot about Sam entirely as I turned in a circle, looking around me.

"What is this place?" I said aloud.

"This is like walking into another country," Birdman agreed. Even he seemed awed by it, pausing for a moment to glance around.

On either side of our cirque, great-mouthed canyons spiraled away, ridges marching down to an unseen valley floor two thousand feet below. Patches of snow were flung on the hillsides like crumpled sheets. The sky hovered above me, nearly close enough to touch, the sun a pale smudge behind sullen clouds. There were no signs of anyone else living, no sign that anyone had ever been here.

We stood in a row. I could see what I was thinking reflected in their faces. We were so small, so insignificant. We were no giants. We were no match for this place.

"We're so close to the sky," Sam said, and he was right. Down by the ocean, whatever churned up above us was so far away that it took a while to make itself known: rain, snow, wind. Here, there was nothing to buffer us.

"That way," Birdman said. Slipping through a fortress of cliffs, passing through a slot that barely let us through, we finally stood on the island's backbone. A row of nameless dark-skinned mountains made up a bumpy spine that stretched for fifty miles end to end. Here was where the snow made up its mind, falling more heavily on one side of the mountains than the other. Here was where water flowed in both directions to the sea, falling through cliffs and glaciers and into the big rivers that flowed to the ocean, rivers that salmon could smell from somewhere way out in the sea. Here was the difference between what I knew and what I would find out.

Along one flank, the way we had come, the long ropy muscle of Turn Back Strait ran for more than a hundred miles east and west, more like river than ocean, finally dumping into the sea at Icy Bay. Along the way it was joined by the surge of Betrayal Sound, a freight train of flood tide that rushed into the bays and drained back out again like pulling a plug.

This was the birthplace of storms, each one lined up in the Gulf of Alaska like shots in a rifle. The clouds, heavy with moisture and lashed by gales, dropped two hundred inches of rain on this side of the island, washing it down with such force that half-grown trees uprooted and slid to the water hundreds of feet below, a soupy mixture of mud and forest. Gashes broke the island's skin at these places, thick brown earth like blood oozing down where trees had been.

I paused, trying to read the landscape. The way we were headed, down the island's meaty thigh, was where the lake hid from us. A band of sheer, slick cliffs circled the mountain we stood on, jutting out into the pale sky. Leaning over, I could see that the rock was split into deep grooves like folds of a blanket. Far below, low trees grew in tortured clumps. Snow still lingered in the shaded places, a layer of slippery white icing.

I waited, hoping for a sign. Nothing moved below me but an eagle, hunting among the cliffs. Hugging the thermals, it floated, its white head standing out in sharp relief in the blur of green and gray. It dove finally, vanishing from sight.

We followed, dropping off the divide and threading through the rocks in a tight passage that only Birdman could figure out. Climbing down slowly through the crumbling cliffs, we reached another hanging valley shaped like the palm of an upturned hand. Spindly yellow poppies, miniature suns, dotted the soft carpet of heather under my feet. A field of purple lupine scented the air with a sweet fragrance. This was a tiny garden, an enchanted, secret place.

The country, gentle now, rolled toward a basin lined with stark gray rock. The walls of the basin slanted sharply down to something unseen.

It had to be the lake. Without a spoken thought, we all paused where we stood. I wondered if the others, like me, had secretly believed that we could not walk here, that my father had been right. But here we were. What was I about to find out?

Birdman wrapped his scarf tightly around his neck. "Go ahead," he said. "Go first." He put a hand on Sam's arm when Sam tried to follow. "This is her place to see first." He gave me a gentle shove. "Go on, girl. We'll be fifteen minutes behind you."

I left them standing there talking in low voices. As I walked, I briefly noticed little things: Clumps of heather with fragile flowers only an inch wide huddled in the lee of the wind. A plant Uncle Dean had sketched for me once called sky pilot, a plant I had always associated with him, which grew only in the most inhospitable high places. Patches of wind-hardened snow, crusted to a shiny patina. A small pond shaped like an eye, surrounded by a scattering of lichen-covered rocks. Ragged patches of blue in the looming sky, more sucker holes. The light touch of rain beading up on my head, almost too light to be rain but something else instead, a kiss, a sigh.

As I reached the edge of the basin, my pace slowed. I had dreamed about this place for so long and I was walking up on it so fast. A part of me wanted to keep it the way it had been: a blue dot on a map, a story of a man and a cabin and blueberries.

I took one step and then another. Finally I dropped over the lip of the basin, and I was there.

Thirteen

The Lake of the Fallen Moon was not beautiful. Small and slate-gray, it huddled in a basin of sharp, dark rock. Saw-toothed cliffs guarded its edges. There was nothing soft about it. It was lonely, windswept, and barren.

Still caught in the grip of winter, ice plastered half of its irregular surface. Snow lingered in grimy banks along the slopes. A low blanket of moss covered the ridge above where I stood. A few stunted trees clung to life in a scattered patch. They all leaned in one direction, as if trying to escape the constant wind.

I thought of our stories of Uncle Dean and his cabin, the blueberries and ice cream. In the stories the lake was a shimmering blue, caressed by gentle winds. Trees grew there. Not these ugly dwarfed creatures but tall and sheltering trees where we would rest. In our stories the weather was warm enough to strip down to the last layer of clothing we wore. Warm enough to float on our backs even, like otters. Even though we knew it couldn't be true, we had also decided it never rained at the Lake of the Fallen Moon. Now I knew that we had dreamed up a completely different place, nothing like this one.

She was not here. She had never been here.

Frantic, I ran clumsily around the lake until I was stopped by cliffs and snow. "Mother!" I called, my voice a ragged echo off the cliffs. I ran, hoping that I had missed some important clue, a tent tucked away in a nook, a fire. I ran, once falling on something hard. I could feel blood running down my leg, but I jumped up without looking, my hair falling into my eyes, my too-big pants twisting around my legs. Finally I slumped to the ground.

Cold seeped slowly through my clothes and I shivered but didn't move. I was a statue, cemented in place. Clouds scooted briskly across the lead-colored sky, on their way to somewhere. Leftover rain drizzled on my face, the remnants of another endless shower.

"Where are you?" I called. My voice echoed around the cliffs again. There was no answer.

On the far side of the lake, bear tracks punctured the snow in a loping gait. They were deep and big, a boar. Maybe the one chasing the sow and cubs around, pushing them higher than they wanted to be.

"Hide, mother bear," I whispered to wherever she was now. But I knew that this was an ancient story; it would spool out the way it always had. Either the mother and cubs would be wily enough to escape, to hole up somewhere, or they wouldn't. There was nothing I could do. It was the way the world worked.

My bones ached, deep in a place I could not name. My knee was swollen, hot to the touch, hurt from whatever I had fallen on. She was not here. Maybe she was in town, somehow improbably passing through all the obstacles with some kind of magic. Maybe, despite what Sam believed, she had already hopped on a crab boat bound for a different place. She could be anywhere. Maybe she had never made it this far at all.

I watched the ice move around on the lake, pushed by the wind. It piled up in large transparent slices on one end, shattering as pieces broke with a tinkling sound. Then the wind would come from a different direction and the ice would scoot across the lake again, some chunks submerging below the surface and others breaking apart. It seemed restless, a constant war of water. Too thin to step on, too cold to swim across, the lake would never be a place of refuge.

I was so tired. It seemed like years since I had left Floathouse Bay. Weariness burned through my veins like a strong drug. It would be easy to sink into this barren ground and sleep forever. The snow would drift over me, the wind eddying around me as it blew across the basin. Was this how my father had felt, poised on the brink between dock and sea?

I would not be like him. I knew that I could not sit here and let the world get the best of me. *There's always some reason to get up in the morning.* I had to find that reason.

When I pulled myself up to stand, I heard something big approaching with a clatter of rocks and the thud of footfalls.

The bear. I turned slowly.

But it wasn't the bear. It was Sam, with Birdman a few steps behind him.

I walked to meet them.

Sam squinted across the lake. "Is she here? Did you find her?"

"No. She's not here. She's not anywhere. I was so sure she would be here."

Sam sighed.

"If she isn't here, then where is she?" he wondered aloud.

"We aren't ever going to find her, are we?" I asked.

"I don't know. Maybe we aren't."

Birdman turned in a circle, hunting for prints. There were none. There should have been some. Already ours took up most of the narrow space between tundra and lake, although I knew it was possible to pass through this type of country without leaving a sign. We all knew how to do it. You kept to the short bristly plants that would not bend. You clung to the copperbush. You stayed on rocks instead of land. You erased yourself with each step.

"No sign," Birdman said.

"I know you believed she was here," Sam added.

"I believed everything they told me," I said. "That we were the best people on the coast, and everyone else was crazy or against us or both. That how we lived was the best, most honest way to live. That she wanted me to find her." I felt the pain of it deep in my heart, my stomach, even my toes.

Birdman set down his pack. He pulled a bandanna from it and held it out to me. "Cold air makes your eyes sting. Does it to me every time."

Sam gently put an arm around my shoulders. His body cut the wind and I did not move away. I could feel the beat of his heart through all the clothes he wore. Slow, steady, just like he had always seemed to be.

"Why not just tell the truth?" I asked in a voice that seemed too fragile for this place. "There are no maps that the salmon read, just some homing instinct that nobody really knows about. Uncle Dean is under the sea somewhere. My father meant to hurt us, because it let out whatever hurt he had inside of him. Why not just say it?"

Sam let out his breath, and I could feel it all the way down the length of his body. "Stories make life a little easier to take sometimes," he said. "What do you think, Birdman?"

Birdman shrugged. "Don't know if anything makes life easier. Life is damn hard and don't let anyone tell you different. But I do know it's getting cold, and it will be dark soon. We'd best make a move if we're going to."

"We could night hike," Sam said. "We've got headlamps, there will be a moon. Our feet will feel the way."

Even though night hiking was dangerous, none of us wanted to be here at night in this strange and desperate place. Even the red cliffs would be better than this. Even dropping off the other side of the lake into the unknown would be better than this.

I stared out over the lake as the others waited for me to decide. "Uncle Dean flew over this lake," I said. "He's the one who told us about it. He made it sound like paradise. There's no blueberry patches like he said there would be."

Birdman kicked aside a patch of snow and examined the thick mat of vegetation beneath. "Might be, in summer. The low bushes, the sweetest tasting of all."

I bent down to look. The straggly bushes looked nothing like the blueberries I knew, but something like hope bubbled up. Maybe there was a strand of truth buried in every story.

"I want to stay," I said impulsively. "We can build a fire to stay warm and leave in the morning."

"You're not quite done with this lake," Birdman said, and I nodded. What if she came back in the night, drawn in by our voices? I could not leave yet.

He surveyed the clumps of trees, scattered across the tundra as though thrown by a giant hand. "Old, old trees," he said. "See how they shut everything down but one strip of heartwood? We'll have to collect what they've shed; it will be good fire starter. We can build a small fire, but the trees won't give us any more than that."

We crunched through the snow bringing back handfuls of twigs and bark. Birdman crouched to strike a match. As the fire blossomed to life, Sam trudged off to fill our water bottles. He did not look back.

"I want to change my name," I said to Birdman. "I want it to be something other than a thing that kills."

"What shall we call you?"

I thought for a moment. "I'm not sure yet."

I knew Birdman had been called by at least one other name long ago. "Take your time," he said. "It'll come to you. You've got years to get it right."

"Why are you called Birdman?" I knew I was treading into dangerous territory. For a moment I expected him to retreat into silence, but he checked to make sure that Sam was still crouched by the lake, bottles lined up beside him. Then he said, "When I was over there, in that place, I used to watch the birds. There were so many different kinds, and I didn't know their names. Wading birds that looked like they walked on stilts, warblers, cormorants. Even odd little ones that only came out at night. I used to wish I could be like them, to fly the hell away from that place."

"Me too," I whispered. "The cormorants. I used to watch them and think that too."

He nodded and went on, "The guys noticed and gave me that name. I didn't mind much, it was better than some I could have gotten. When I came back my old name didn't really fit anymore. So now I go by Birdman. It reminds me of that place, but not in a bad way."

We watched Sam pace the lakeshore, a stream of pebbles falling through his hands. He was only a shadow now, and the lake beside him was black marble.

"Birdman, I want to forgive him. Can you teach me how?"

He said, "Face to face with a bear, that moment of mutual recognition, it's a powerful thing. Who can say what any of us would have done?"

I imagined myself in the alder tunnels, a rifle clutched in sweaty hands. The screams of the cruisers were a tinny echo in comparison to my father's cries. The bear saw me and hesitated. Only moments stood between us and the crunch of bone. The urge for self-preservation was strong, stronger than blood.

Would I have run?

"I might have run," I said. I stared into the fire so that I would not have to meet Birdman's eyes. But he said, "I might have run too."

"You would never run. You're never afraid."

I could feel him thinking for a moment, making a decision. "I did run," he said. "I ran, plain and simple, from Angela. Never paid a dime to her mother. I know all about the wilderness but not so much about keeping promises."

His eyes were brimming full in the firelight. It could have been the smoke. It could have been something else.

"After we get home, I am going to look for her. I really will this time. I'll find her and make things right. You think she'll slam the door in my face?"

"She won't," I said, although I was not sure.

"I ran one other time," Birdman said. His voice was so low I had to strain to hear it. "Back there, in that place. It was a calm day, it had been quiet for days, not the spooky kind of quiet that meant they were sneaking around looking for us, but real quiet like we were the only ones out there. I almost believed it, that we were safe, the worst was over. We were all kind of trash talking, joking, not thinking. We walked right into an ambush because I hadn't been looking for sign like I was supposed to. I got too used to it, that quiet. I felt pretty good that day, and there were lots of birds, not like in some of the places where the planes were spraying. Flat missed the signs, looking at birds. Then all hell broke loose, guys were being mowed down and all I could think was, how the hell can I get out of here and stay alive? So I ran. In the confusion nobody saw. There were guys running all over the place anyway. Plenty of places to hide, maybe some other guys did it too, I don't know. After it got quiet again I crept back out of my hiding place back there in the tules and found all the guys dead or close to, all except Isaiah, and he was barely alive. I heard the chopper coming and I crawled in that mess like I had been there all along. Just got lucky, I told the medics, a bunch of the guys fell on me and I didn't get a scratch. They all believed me, why would I make that up? That's the real story. That's what really happened. My fault, those deaths heavy on my heart, all of these years. I can remember all of them, Joey and Wild Bill and Harper, faces just as clear as yours is now."

"You didn't mean for them to die," I whispered.

He shrugged. "Doesn't matter, the end was the same."

"Does Isaiah know?"

"I guess he does. I started to talk about it once, years ago, and he made me stop. Said it didn't matter what had happened in that place. We were friends then and would always be friends."

The fire chewed its way through the wood of trees older than either of us put together. The silence between us was different now. It settled around us like an old, comfortable blanket.

"All of us carry something we're not proud of," Birdman said finally. "You, me, Sam. Roy too. Live long enough, you're bound to be carrying something."

I reached out and gathered Birdman's hands in mine for just a second, as long as he would allow. "Thank you for telling me."

"It's been years since I've talked about this," he said, pulling his coat tighter against the chill. "Last thing I want is to be one of those guys who have their feet planted in the past. Better to hold this deep in the gut where it can't come out." He indicated Sam, heading back to us. "Keep this under your hat. Don't need the world knowing my secrets. You, I trust with them."

Sam sat down beside me, close enough to touch if I wanted. He held his hands out over the fire. "Water's the coldest I ever felt," he said. "Burned me, almost, it's that cold."

"Look," I said. In the sliver of lake without ice, the reflection of a perfect full moon glistened in the black depths.

"Lake of the Fallen Moon," I whispered.

It was beautiful.

"Won't be a good night," Birdman said in a gruff voice. "Moon's no good for sleeping." I could see that he thought he had gone too far in his telling, and he had to retreat for a while. I knew that something other than the moon would keep him awake. He rose stiffly to his feet and limped over to his bedroll. I knew he wasn't going to be sleeping—from the light of the fire, flickering on his face, I could see his eyes, wide open.

Sam looked at me and away again quickly. "After we climb down from here you may never want to see me again. If that happens, I can charter a plane and be on my way. Just say the word."

When I thought about watching Sam step on a floatplane and fly out of the bay, my heart ached a little bit. He was nothing like the man my mother would have chosen for me. He had none of the confidence and swagger that had propelled my father through life. He did not have the woods sense of Birdman or the cheerful glow that Isaiah had. With Sam, there was only the sense of slipping deep into a hot springs pool, my body unclenching like a closed fist. That had to add up to something worth trying.

"Don't go right away," I said. "Stay one season at least. Stay until the whales come back." I was about to add one more word: *Promise*. I caught it before it left my lips. There had been enough promises.

"We might still find her," he said. "Alaska's like that. You don't see people for years and they suddenly pop up again. Happens every day."

He could be right, but in my heart I knew that my mother belonged out here, somewhere in this fragile and beautiful country. Not for her a sore-footed life working at a diner, cleaning fish on a slime line. Her hair cut short, her heart broken. Maybe it was better for her to disappear into this place, let it wrap its arms around her forever.

"I'm alone," I said, the idea sinking in for the first time. We had been so busy setting up our camp and gathering firewood that it had stayed at bay, something lurking out there in the darkness. Now it moved in on me, bottomless as the lake. Both of my parents were gone. I was alone without a map to guide me.

Sam reached over with one hand and let it rest for a moment on mine before he moved it away. "You know I thought about you.

Every day that you were gone I thought about you. But I didn't want to just be your escape route. That's why I didn't show up in Float-house Bay the year you left. I was waiting for you to come back on your own. I was waiting for you to choose me."

"I had to choose myself first," I said, and I realized it was true. To break free of the currents that trapped me in Never Summer, I had to go and learn that there were other ways to live. I had to make my own way instead of stepping in to someone else's footprints.

"Fair enough." But Sam still looked troubled. He fidgeted, pushing his hair off his face, carefully piling another load of branches on the fire. For a moment the smoke obscured the space between us.

"Is anything possible between us, after what I told you?" he asked me at last.

Here was where I got to choose. I could hold on to my sorrow the way my mother had, turning her life into a web of half-truths. I could let it spiral out into a forever anger the way my father had done. Or I could do something different.

"Look at where we are," I said. The moon reflecting on the lake, the silent mountains overhead. Could I have dreamed this up only a day ago? "Isn't it easy to think that anything's possible?"

When I looked at him I did not see the man I had first loved, someone I had been drawn to because he was slow like a river past snowmelt, water I could see through clear to the sand beneath. I loved him then because he was not like my father. I was beginning to love him now for a different reason, for the real man I was start-ing to know. His shoulders were slumped with weariness and he had long ago lost any spark he once had as a younger man, but sometimes I could see it in his eyes, a coal waiting to be kindled. What else was left for me to know?

In the morning, frost coated our sleeping bags and painted the long grass as silver as an old woman's hair. A fine, light snow the consistency of sugar had fallen late in the night, so late that none of us had seen it.

The fire steamed and hissed in the chilly air. My breath was a cloudburst. The calendar had clicked over to spring, but it was forever winter here. Nobody could stay up here for long. It was time to go lower, where real people could live.

"Sam?" I said, and he came to sit on his heels beside me, handing over coffee. "Tell me about the whales."

"What about them?"

"You said that they didn't sing the same songs. How did you know that?"

He dropped down to sit cross-legged next to me, bringing his own cup from near the fire. "Spent a lot of time reading books on anchor watch. Not a lot else to do, just listen to the slap of water on the hull, clients snoring. This one book I read said that there are three different kinds of whales in the ocean. They call them the transients, those are the kinds that just pass through, and then there's the residents, the ones we used to see feeding in Never Summer all the time. And there's this other kind, a kind nobody knows much about, called the offshores. You wouldn't know it by looking at them, but none of the three kinds cross each other's lines, and they don't speak the same language."

"I never knew," I said. For years my mother and I watched the rounded backs of whales as they passed by our bay. We had seen them hunt off the far shores. The whales almost seemed like they were somehow related to us, familiar cousins we saw once a year. There had been no mystery about them.

"Sam?" I asked. "Do you think anybody ever knows all there is to know?" As I said it I knew I sounded less like a woman and more like a child, but the words slipped out anyway.

Sam didn't laugh. He blew on his cup of coffee even though mine had cooled enough to sip. "I think you can know an awful lot about some things," he said. His wave indicated Birdman, who was puttering around the edge of our campsite, shoving his sleeping bag into his pack. "Birdman knows all about tracks and who left them and sometimes why. The rest of him is locked up tight some-place. Roy knew a lot about the ocean, and about bears. But every-thing? No. I think you have to pick and choose what you want to know. That has to be enough."

I wasn't sure if that would ever be enough. It seemed to me that if you knew all the secrets, you would never pick the wrong path. But then I realized people were not the same as salmon, or even whales. Even if there were a map to show us where to go, a foolproof route that would get us home, some of us would not follow it. We would be seduced into other rivers. We would chase flashier fish into different waters. We would spin elaborate tales to make up for the gaps in our lives.

"Sam?" I asked again. "How do I know, if we're in the desert or in the mountains, or anywhere, and things go wrong, that you won't run?"

Sam clutched his mug, fingers gone white. He had forgotten his gloves somewhere, I thought. "Well, Winnie, I don't know. I've been a nomad all my life. I can try to nail my feet to one place. I can try my best. I can promise you that."

Promises. Would I ever be able to hear that word again without remembering? But then coffee as warm as love trickled down my throat. I could feel it spread through all of the veins and arteries of my body. Bitter grounds caught in my teeth like grains of sand and I laughed.

Sam looked at me, puzzled. "This coffee is terrible," I said. "You didn't learn that from my father. His was high octane, to get every-one moving, remember? He did that on purpose. I used to think he ran on coffee, that and cigars. At least tell me you'll try to make better coffee."

He laughed too. "Coffee. Okay, we can start with that." It was good to see him throw back his head, grinning, and the smile lines around his eyes, seen too seldom. I was right: there was a spark there after all. Maybe I could be the one to bring that fire back to life. Maybe it would be a different kind of fire than the one my father had burned with, maybe the kind of enduring flame that did not blow out in a capricious wind. In the end there were many kinds of fire, just as there were many kinds of tide and many kinds of people. I felt a little bubble of excitement at the thought. There was still so much to find out.

We gathered up our camp, stopping often to blow on chapped fingers. The cold knifed its way through my coat and I hurried, punching the contents of my pack down so I could close it. Winter hovered over us like a fourth person in our group, icing up our tarp lines and freezing the water in our canteens to a solid block.

Birdman always packed up in a set of fluid movements, much faster than we could. He had a system of where everything went in his pack, unlike Sam and me, and he was shifting from foot to foot as we finished stuffing items away.

"It's time to get back to the ocean where we belong," he said. "We could go on from here, try to walk into town, but I don't think we'll find anything, if we've seen nothing here. I would do it though, for you."

I looked across the snowfield, unbroken by any tracks save the bear's. "Which way would we go?"

He waved an arm to the east. "Over there, around the lake, where it drops off. Posthole through the snow and traverse to the cliff you can barely see. We'd climb down the place where the water's carved a trough in the stone, and follow that to the cedar flats below. From there, we could find deer trails that would take us to town. Two days, three, tops."

I felt the route tug at me. Maybe we could keep walking after all. We could be the people who made it. We might find more ribbons swaying on the trees farther below. We might find tracks in the sands of the lower valleys, the ashes of campfires in the trees. At the same time, I knew we would be risking our lives. We would run short of food and time, a stack of bones scattered by animals, our hair bound up in birds' nests. Disappearing forever, just like so many had done before us. I knew my mother would not wish that for me. I knew, too, that she was really and truly gone.

"We'll do whatever you want," Sam said. I could tell by the way he stood, poised beside his pack, that he wanted to go back the way that was familiar. Despite the cabin in the aspens he had talked of, he would always be a man who felt safer in the landscape he knew. That he offered to travel a path that was unknown said more about him than any words of repentance or love ever could.

For a brief moment I was reminded of standing in a swaying boat, ready to pull the starter cord, my mother waiting for me to choose. Moments like this crept up on a person without warning. You were never prepared to make the choices that could change your life forever.

"I want to go back," I said, and I realized it was true. "I want to go back to Never Summer Bay."

Sam and Birdman shouldered their packs. They began to walk across the basin but stopped when they saw that I had not moved.

"I'll catch up," I told them. "Just give me a minute."

Birdman nodded, understanding this more than anyone. He marched away across the hanging valley to stay out of sight. I knew he would hunker down to give his knees a break and that when I walked up to find him, he would show me the best way to go home.

"I'll give you all the time you need," Sam said. "I'll just wait over in the trees. I'll wait a long time, if I have to."

I knew he was talking about more than just the minute that I stood here with the lake at my back. I knew that he meant some approximation of forever. I leaned into his warm body for a second, long enough to let him know that every trouble could be unraveled and smoothed out with enough time. Then I walked closer to the lake and looked in.

In the night a light skin of ice had formed over the lake. Soon it would look like nobody had ever been there. The ashes of our fire would sink into the soil. Our footprints would fill with rain and snow, becoming mere suggestions of tracks. Soon, more snow would fall, heavy and deep, covering everything.

"Lake of the Fallen Moon," I whispered. For my mother and me, it had been a different sort of place, a holy grail where life was easy and men landed gently in airplanes. It was something my mother had clung to all the lonely years since Dean had disappeared. Had she really believed he was here all along? Or had she known, deep inside, that his story would never have a happy ending?

My knee throbbed. Something swam up to a conscious thought.

I walked over to where I had fallen the day before. Under the skiff of snow a piece of moss was pulled back from my boot heel striking it. Something hard was under there. Something silver. Something that didn't belong.

Kneeling, I tore off wet moss in handfuls, exposing what lay beneath.

It was the long curve of an airplane wing

None of it really made sense to me. In the ocean, the gray bodies of whales foraged under a clouded sun. They drew up their prey in a net of bubbles. The salmon followed an unwritten map back to their home stream. The bears slept in day beds among the big trees. It was all an endless circle, all of us bound together in a knot that could never really be untied. All we had to count on was what we carried with us, our memories and our hopes for the future. This land was constantly changing, evolving, growing, the same as we were. We had to balance that load between the two, the past and the present, and hope that it was enough.

I had always followed someone else. I followed the thread of her stories, wanting to believe. I followed my father through the estuaries and up the salmon streams. I followed in the steps of bears and along the trails that deer punched through the beach fringe. I never before dared to make my own prints. It always seemed so precarious, each step a walk out onto an uncertain land.

I stood up and took a deep breath that I could feel all the way down to my bones. Then I turned to face a distant sun and headed back home, making my own tracks.

Fourteen

Sam and I have lived in Never Summer Bay for years now, a lifetime. We have grown into each other like moss. He still talks about the desert, the open road, especially on those days when the rain blows sideways, a curtain separating us from any other place in the world. He looks through maps; he paces in long strides across the room. But he never goes. I have begun to believe that he never will.

We have rebuilt parts of the lodge, but mostly we have let the forest have what it wants. It seems better that way, to melt into the trees rather than the way we always did it before.

We have talked deep into the night about babies, little girls with hair almost silver, and someday we may decide. If it happens, we won't name her after a rifle, or the river, or the mountains. She'll have a name she can live up to, something solid yet something that can bend.

I never changed my own name. I meant to, but after a few years it seemed like I needed to hold on to one thing that belonged to the past. Old ghosts can be good ones, after enough time has passed. Sam calls me Win now, and that is close enough.

We never found my mother. Maybe we were wrong in turning back by Lake of the Fallen Moon. Maybe we should have continued on, down to the place where the avalanches roared in spring, drinking from the sweet chill of all the waterfalls, cutting steps in the shrink-ing glaciers, and finally reaching town. Maybe we could have done it, despite all the odds stacked against us. Maybe that is what she did, although if anyone in town knows her, they aren't saying.

There is one thing I would like to ask her. Sometimes, late at night when I lean against Sam's back, love like a slow current of a deep river passing between us, I wonder if her leaving was her final gift to my father. Though it is difficult to imagine, she must have known that he could not survive in a world without big trees, and even more, a world in which he was not the same man he wanted himself to be. I wonder if she left because she knew that her van-ishing was the only way he would have the courage to release the brake on the chair.

I will never know the answer.

Our lodge is a happy place where families come in by floatplane, chubby toddlers and wide-eyed parents, all hoping to see bears. They are from places like Indiana and New Jersey, and as far removed from the old bear hunting clients as they can possibly be.

They tiptoe through this strange place instead of trying to own it. We teach them about the circle of life, salmon and bears and trees, and we hope that some of it sticks.

Birdman sometimes comes over for a few days and shows them tracks pressed firmly into damp sand, and the kids all love him and cry when he leaves. They call him the Alaska Santa because of his big beard, and I think he likes the name.

His gaze sometimes lingers on the little girls with cinnamon-colored hair. Angela has never come to Floathouse Bay, and he does not look for her. "Someday," he says, but with each year that goes by he says it less and less.

Isaiah never comes to our bay. He says that the memories are too hard for him to work his way through. He likes his peace in

Floathouse Bay and says the only way he will leave is when he is carried out feet first. Instead Sam and I travel the distance between us and him often, piloting our boat past all of God's cargo pockets. We sit on the dock and sip liquid that burns all the way down our throats, and we talk about the old days and the days to come. Sometimes we swim, though I never open my eyes underwater. I don't want to know what lies beneath.

The coast seems smaller now than it ever was. We are part of a loose network of people who have chosen to live here for our own reasons, and we talk back and forth by radio telephone and on the marine channels. We share everything now. The new couple at the fish weir sends slabs of salmon to us; we bundle up our old magazines and newspapers that our clients leave with us for them. We share fuel and food and bodies to help search for the missing. It is a better way to live.

If anyone speaks of my father now it is filtered through years of forgetting. They talk about how he ran a boat as though it was part of his body rather than a man-made piece of fiberglass and steel. They talk about the storms he taunted and the narrow escapes he made. They raise their glasses in salute. He is a legend now, just the way he would have liked it. Nobody mentions the other side of him anymore.

There is only one reason why I cannot forget that side of him, and that reason is all tangled up in Enchantment Bay. What was begun in Enchantment Bay is a story that is not yet finished. It is a story involving wood and desire and what some people call progress.

Ernie tells us that the loggers are on their way. Sometimes I think I can hear the whine of their saws, although Sam tells me it is only the wind. It will be years before they get here, he tells me, and by then we will be dead and buried under the muskeg. I want to believe him, I really do.

Sometimes we sit on the dock in summer, and I can feel the red cliffs breathing above us. I try not to look too deep into the water for fear of what I might see. Instead I look across the sparkling surface, watching only what lies above.

I remember one thing that I had long since forgotten. Days Uncle Dean disappeared, my father went out alone searching. Did he go to the red cliffs? He never told us if he climbed to the lake, or if he found pieces of a silver plane. I often wonder if he did. Sitting on the dock that last night, the ashes of a fire swallowed by tide, did he realize that I would soon discover what had been left behind? I have so many questions I would like to ask him, but that is the one I hold closest to my heart.

On other nights I think of Lake of the Fallen Moon and what secrets it still holds. I think of the salmon circling in the ocean, following their own map home, and of all the things that I don't know and never will know.

I listen for the whales and wait for them to come back to our bay. The ones who pass through might be the unpredictable transients, trying out new bays as they travel the coast. They might be the residents, seeking the familiar and the safe. They might be the elusive offshores, about which little is known. There is no way to tell, so I listen for them all. I try to learn what it is that they want me to know.